the Lover's Surrender

J.C. REED

Cover art by Larissa Klein

Editing by Therin Knite

ISBN: 1519443609
ISBN-13: 978-1519443601

To all who love and are loved:

Love is a wild ride. Without the passion, we wouldn't surrender and conquer what we never thought could be ours. True love stories don't have happy endings, because for those who treasure it, true love never ends.

- J.C. Reed

New York City

STALKING WASN'T DANNY'S forte. He was used to his men doing this job for him, watching victims for endless hours, prepared to strike the moment those victims were vulnerable.

Cushioned in the fake perception of safety.

However, today's victim was an exception. There was something special about the woman he was observing.

Her brown hair, long and curly, and her face, now tanned with freckles, reminded him too much of a girl he had once dated. Brooke Stewart was in every way the carbon copy of her elder sister Jenna, now dead.

3

Jenna had been a good prostitute, he remembered, the way she could take his whole cock in her mouth, and suck him to pleasure heaven. At least she admitted she was a whore, as all women were, and whores needed to be shown the way.

Defeated when they were taken.

Controlled when they were too wild.

Too bad he had turned her into a user, stealing his drugs when he was out of it. If she hadn't been so stupid as to take what wasn't hers, she might still be alive.

The first time Danny suspected Jenna had been stealing was when a bag of high-end drugs had gone missing from his place. The second time it happened, it was time to sell her, if only to make up for his lost revenue.

And sell her good he did.

First came his friends, and then he started to look for buyers. The money Jenna earned him was good, way better than what he made as a small-town drug dealer. Back then, in the beginning, she hadn't even been aware of how easily he could spike her drink without her knowing, and then invite five to ten guys a night to have their way with her.

The bruises all over her body, he explained, were there because she was too thin. High on drugs, she didn't even feel the pain. And what Jenna couldn't remember never happened, and the fragments of memories she dreamed were just a figment of her imagination.

Danny smiled fondly.

It had been a win-win situation for the both of them, he remembered. In some way, she started his career as her pimp. However, the real turning point came when one of his richer clients wanted her. Not just for one hour or a night, but as a possession, as a slave that he could keep in a cage—to do with as he pleased.

Thirty thousand dollars had been the price he had offered Danny. It sounded like a good deal at first…until his client explained he wanted Jenna for a club he was a member of. Needless to say, Danny began to think of Jenna as a long-term investment. She could make him way more money as a prostitute, so he declined. Weeks passed. He had almost forgotten about the deal when a bigger offer came in.

One hundred thousand dollars.

It was so much money, Danny almost caved in on the spot, but he wasn't ready to sell her just yet. He figured if someone was willing to pay such an exorbitant sum of money—more than three times the initial offer—he'd probably offer more. It was a good thing he had listened to his little birdie, because the next thing he knew he received an offer that changed his life:

One million dollars for his girl.

Plus a ten percent discount for whatever drugs they supplied to him. And the guarantee that he had protection from the police.

But the one condition?

Work for the secret organization called ETNAD, an extensive elite club run by high-ranked and rich individuals, and keep quiet about it. It was an offer too good to be passed on.

Oh, how good a businessman he was.

Oh, what a time it had been.

Another chuckle escaped his mouth, and he licked his lips.

It was the beginning of a symbiotic working relationship with the ETNAD club. They had made him rich beyond his wildest dreams, rewarding him for his consistency and loyalty. They had made him the owner of a nightclub and given him the kind of power he had always dreamed of.

Now, ten years later, he drove four expensive cars, owned four houses, and had his own men working for him. He made so much money that he could easily buy a small island, and someday he would…once it was time to retire.

He was no longer a cheap lowlife.

In all the years he had worked for ETNAD, with the exception of a few he could count on his hand, he hadn't seen a single one of the girls he had provided again. He never asked what happened to them, and he didn't want to know. His lifestyle was too grand, too exquisite to allow the kind of consequences that came with being inquisitive.

After all, when he sold the girls, they became the buyer's possession, their property.

But there were rumors and clues hard to miss. Eventually, he found out that the girls were raped, tortured, many of them killed for pleasure.

The shock lasted all of a second.

He had always guessed that with so much money involved, illegal events had to be at play; that the motivation behind ETNAD's diligence was to keep the clandestine trade running smoothly.

It didn't take long for them to suspect Danny's knowing about their little secret.

Danny remembered that day all too well. It had been exactly five years, six months, and ten days ago when they first asked him if he would be interested in taking part in a private party.

It wasn't exactly a question, but a test.

What choice did he have but to say yes, if only to please them and grow his already prosperous relationship with them?

It wasn't so much the money he earned that instantly persuaded him to jump in. It was their guarantee that he could do what he wanted and get away it. It was the knowledge that they had the power and the connections to make everything disappear. And when they prospered, his profits increased, too.

And so his first attendance became one of several invitations that now came with the job.

Oh, how much he wanted to do it again. To relive the memories.

He prided himself on how powerful he felt. To know that it took almost nothing to kill someone, like a wild animal could kill its prey without any consequences. To have the power to decide over life and death. To know that nothing could touch him.

But then, he had slogged hard for his money.

Yes, there were times he felt sorry that Jenna was gone. After all, she was the very first of many whores who worked for him. Drug addiction aside, she had been a good girl, and naïve, the way only a fifteen-year-old could be. Foolish as she had been, she had been in love with him. There was never a doubt she would have done anything he wanted.

However, business was business. Love had no place in a world ruled by money, sex, and power. And power was something he now lived for. That Jenna was killed was just a part of a business transaction—a sacrifice that had been necessary to ensure his lifestyle. After all, only the fittest survived, and he was as tough as one could be.

It had all started with that one girl, Jenna. Brooke's sister. What an irony that it would end with Brooke.

When he first saw Jenna's younger sister a little over

three months ago, he couldn't believe that Brooke was the same girl he had met ten years ago—the very same woman, who brought a hell of a lot of trouble to him that year, when she escaped ETNAD.

Of course he knew she'd fight to get justice for her sister, knowing that Danny was to blame for her death. But how the fuck did she dare go against him? How did she dare run away from him, after he worked so hard to get where he was?

He balled his hands as unwanted memories began to flood his mind.

Now he wished he had been harder on her.

If he had done his job right, then Brooke would never have escaped his claws after ETNAD had her abducted. He wouldn't have run into trouble with his boss. And when Dante was angry, that was never a good thing.

So, when he stopped his car in front of Brooke's building and saw that her lights were switched on, he smiled. She was there, all alone. Waiting for him. Or not waiting, but surely she could feel his presence, maybe even feel apprehension at the knowledge that she couldn't get away from him.

A ringing noise disrupted his train of thoughts. He picked up his phone, his eyes not leaving the woman he was watching from inside his car, which he had conveniently parked in front of Brooke's building.

"What's the status?" the voice on the other end asked as a means of introduction. Danny recognized the voice immediately. It belonged to one of the many low-ranked guys working for ETNAD. He didn't call them friends because Danny had none. During the hard life he had lived, he had learned to only trust himself.

"Good. Couldn't be better."

"And the envelope?"

"Delivered. By now Brooke knows that Dante is out and has turned away from her boyfriend."

"Did anyone see you?"

Danny frowned. "Since when do I play courier? Obviously, one of my men made sure it got delivered."

Or, more precisely, his cousin Barrow had.

"She's here, all alone in her apartment, you know?" Danny's voice rose with excitement. "I could strike this instant. Now that she's all alone, I could go up. It would be easy. Just give me the order and I'll take care of her."

"No need. Dante has plans for her, " the other voice said. "He wants you to focus on Mayfield first."

"Mayfield's already been taken care of. I think we should take her now."

"She isn't the problem."

What the fuck? Danny held the phone away from his ear to curse, then returned, quiet and calm.

"She escaped. And she knows too much. How can that

not be a problem?"

"According to Dante, she isn't."

Oh Dante.

How he hated that arrogant motherfucking asshole known as Nate. But, in spite of his annoyance with his boss, Danny didn't dare reveal his true thoughts.

"What does he need the bitch for anyway?" Danny asked instead. "The first job is done. I was able to separate her from Mayfield. She doesn't trust him, so I can easily get to her now. In a few hours, I'll call the police, and Mayfield will be accused of killing the girl I took care of yesterday. Now would be a good time to take Brooke away. This is my professional opinion."

"Not now," the guy on the line said stubbornly. "Dante's order. He wants you to focus on Mayfield, and nothing but Mayfield. Make sure he gets arrested tomorrow. How you do it is your problem. As for the girl, you had your chance at the club. Dante knows about your failure, so he's changed his mind about Brooke."

Danny balled his hand into a fist.

Failure.

He hated that word.

Yes, he had been so close to her at the club. She'd already been drugged. And then her asshole boyfriend had appeared and ruined his plan.

Stupid whore.

It was all her fault.

He spat on the floor at the knowledge that the little whore had escaped.

"I'm getting there," he whispered. "Do I have permission to enter her boyfriend's premises?"

"Yes. Whatever gets the job done," the voice continued. "As soon as Mayfield is out of the picture, and Dante has access to the company's money and is able to transfer it to an offshore account, he'll disappear. He expects you to tie up all loose ends until then and take care of his problem. And then, only then, can you take care of the girl."

Danny looked up at the window, the thin curtain doing nothing to hide the silhouette of a woman. He knew it was Brooke, all alone up there and clueless. He knew because the moment his cousin had finished interrogating her as part of a fake investigation, Danny had called him, and ever since he had been following Brooke everywhere she went.

The thought of her all naked beneath her clothes aroused him. Oh, what he could do with her. He couldn't wait to get to that part.

She might be his dead girlfriend's sister, but he was certain they shared a connection, and, as such, they had a lot in common.

He chuckled.

Soon.

Very soon he'd wrap his hands around her little throat.

Danny smiled. "Tell him I got it. I'll call when I'm done."

And with that, he hung up and leaned back in thought.

Yes, the first part of his plan had been accomplished. He had separated her from Jett Mayfield. The next step was following orders. To fulfill that, he was going to replace Brooke's belongings with those of her friend—the one he had killed the day before—and then tip off the cops.

It was a brilliant plan, one he had carefully prepared for weeks.

Once Mayfield was out of the picture and Brooke was all alone, with no protection and no one to take care of her, he'd find her, drug her again. Only then, when Mayfield was finally accused of committing murder, could he do what he had immediately wanted upon setting eyes on her.

Rape her. Kill her.

He liked that. Sure, there were obstacles to be removed first. Her boyfriend Jett was one of them, but he had a fucking plan so grand that no one would see it coming before it hit them.

He liked that ability—to plan ahead—about himself.

As a child, he had wanted to be a magician, able to transfix people. What he could do today was far greater. It wasn't magic, but it was just as powerful.

To have the power to scare someone, to make them doubt everything they'd ever believed about themselves, and—the best of the best about his new life—to frame someone else for a murder he committed…oh, how much he enjoyed being in control.

He was a genius.

Too bad the world didn't know of his brilliance.

"There's no way that motherfucker isn't going down," Danny whispered with a new sense of pride.

As soon as he got rid off Jett, he would focus on her. He would show her where she belonged. He smiled, pleased with the thought.

He had earned it.

So his boss hadn't said those exact words.

No big deal.

But Danny was sure Dante would want him to have fun. And even though his boss didn't see his brilliance yet, someday he would understand. Brooke was a temptation, his reward. She belonged to him. She had escaped that one time. But this time, he'd make sure she'd never leave. Maybe he wasn't allowed to have her just yet, but who was to say he couldn't mess with her?

With a smile, he grabbed a pen and began to write down the poem that had been running through his head. He figured as soon as he returned from Jett's apartment, he'd pay the little bitch a visit.

Chapter 1

JETT

New York City, 12 hours previously

I DREW IN a thick breath. My head was buried in my arms, pounding from the pressure inside. For the past thirty minutes, I had been sitting in the silence of the room, trying hard not to think, not to feel, not to do anything. If I moved, I was sure I'd give in to my anger. And once it broke free, I sure as hell wouldn't be able to contain it.

Brooke's words didn't please me.

Scratch that.

The phone conversation with Brooke didn't calm

me…at all.

In fact, if it weren't for my last ounce of self-control, I would have driven off to find the motherfucker who had dared to meet up with her.

The motherfucker who had probably wanted to touch her.

Who might not know that she was my woman.

Brooke Stewart was a sexy woman with eyes the rich color of chestnuts and lips so kissable that she never had to put on makeup to turn herself beautiful.

But fuck, she was as stubborn and fierce as they came, and she was unlike any other woman I'd dated before. Her endless need for answers and her unwillingness to accept a simple explanation often pushed me to the brink of exasperation. Because that's how Brooke was: cautious, mistrusting, and now vengeful—all the result of her difficult past.

Whatever came her way, she questioned.

But now I was dealing with a new set of problems, which included Brooke's ridiculous belief that I was having an affair.

Okay, she hadn't said those exact words, but accusing me of being a cheater and a liar came close enough. However, she couldn't be further from the truth.

She'd drawn her incorrect conclusion after seeing me with Tiffany, one of my best friends, who also happened to be a distant ex in my long list of lovers. It was the beginning of my experience with Brooke turning sour, the lashing out at each other, and there was nothing I could do except explain…and I would be damned if I'd reveal my intentions.

If only my plan hadn't gone wrong in the first place.

If only I hadn't asked Tiffany to bring the engagement ring to the hotel where Brooke and I were staying.

If only I had known my ex still had feelings for me, had known she would kiss me in her drunken state while Brooke was watching.

No idea what she was doing at the bar, or how she found us, but she caught us in a compromising situation and consequently drew her own conclusions.

It didn't matter now. All that mattered was that Brooke was hurting, and, as such, was trying to get back at me. She hadn't said it in those exact words, but there had been no denying it either.

I knew for sure she planned on seeing someone today.

I could hear it in the tone of her voice that carried over the telephone line, the undercurrents slightly shaking with anger and with something else.

Was it revenge?

Was it fear of being found out?

And if it wasn't for her tone betraying her, then definitely the way she said, *"It's none of your business what I do.*

I can do whatever I want," with so much anger, it spoke of hatred.

Good thing I had installed a tracker in her phone, which is how I discovered that she had met with a guy behind my back.

Without it, I would never have known where she was spending the night, or with whom. I would never have found out his address or the fact that he was the owner of Grayson Photography.

Good thing, too, that she was now back at her place. If she hadn't been, I would have stormed into his place and kicked him across the room. Picked her up, dragged her back to my apartment—where she belonged—and locked her up until she came to her senses, in case I didn't find a way to tame that wild heart of hers.

But I would do none of those things.

Not now.

Not tomorrow.

At least, not yet.

I wasn't yet ready to show her how jealous and possessive I was, how the thought of losing her to someone else was killing me slowly from the inside out, while changing me into the kind of person I wasn't.

Someday I would make her mine—legally in black and white.

It was a solemn promise I had made to myself. No

matter the cost.

Money didn't matter; it was to own her, to make her irrevocably mine.

She had captured my heart, and I wasn't going to lose her.

There were days when I didn't recognize myself—like having the urge to protect her from the smallest things just because she was pregnant. Or like the constant impulse to check my cell phone in the hope she'd call. I had to hear her voice to assure myself that it had been me she had been thinking of when she tried to spend the night with a stranger she picked up at a bar—even though that stranger had been me all along.

I recognized it in my need to know she was okay, hoping I could do more than pay off her loans, while ending her doubts about me once and for all.

Then there were the days I could barely fight off the urge to find the ones who hurt her and torture them as they had tried to torture her. To exact revenge and erase the scars for good. It was a part of me that I tried hard to change, a part I kept hidden from Brooke. A part I knew I couldn't control.

It would only be a matter of time until the unpreventable happened. I hoped Brooke wouldn't be there to witness it.

It was almost midnight when faint footsteps echoed

down the hall. I only raised my head when a loud rap echoed from the door.

"Come in," I muttered.

The door opened, and Kenny's head popped in. "I came as soon as I could." He stepped in and closed the door behind him.

His hair was dripping wet. No surprise. It had been either raining or snowing outside for days. November had a tendency to be unpredictable—like my life.

Then again, nothing ever stayed the same in New York. Except for Kenny and his recurrent outbursts of frustration when things weren't the way he expected them to be. His current motive of frustration was his broken wrist and consequent inability to do all the things he usually pursued. He couldn't wait to get rid of the cast he was wearing and resume his somewhat illegal activities as a hacker.

"Man, what a long day. It's been crazy," he said as he carefully shrugged off his jacket, wincing throughout the entire process, and walked over to me. Dark circles dominated his face, overpowering the sky blue color of his eyes. He didn't have to tell me that he was exhausted. The way he slumped down on the couch and sighed loudly told an entire story.

I nodded. "Couldn't agree more."

The moment I brushed off Tiffany's advances, she had disappeared. Less than eight hours ago, Kenny and I had driven to the hotel to look for her and found her comatose on the floor, the countless small bottles around her reminding me of a macabre shrine.

I had no doubt that had we found her a few hours later, she would have been dead.

Her relapse had been nagging at the back of my mind, but compared to my recent confrontation with Brooke and her feelings of betrayal, it was nothing.

Thinking of Tiffany always made me feel guilty.

In the three hours since leaving the hospital, her near death experience hadn't entered my mind. All I could think about was Brooke, and the guy she might or might not be seeing, and what she might do next.

I had changed so much I barely recognized myself.

My friends used to matter to me more than any woman. I had called them my home, my family. Now Brooke consumed my life. As if she was part of my breath. She had become my home, my world. Soon she would be my family.

The only family I ever had.

"How is she?" I asked quietly, more out of need to say something than true interest.

Tiffany was a friend, but she was also a grown-up. I had saved her life. Now it was her choice whether she wanted to turn that life around.

Kenny shrugged. "As good as the circumstances allow." He gave me a quick glance. "They're keeping her locked up for a few days. You know, for observation and all."

I nodded grimly.

I had no positive words left to say about Tiffany. Although she was my friend, I hadn't yet fully forgiven her for the trouble she had caused me.

"Don't beat yourself up," Kenny continued, misinterpreting my silence. "You heard her. She said she was fine."

"Last time, she said the same thing before she crashed," I remarked dryly.

"Doesn't mean you're to blame for her relapse."

"I know that, but..." I sighed. "I regret seeing her. It was a mistake to meet with her, raising her hopes like that, then brushing her off. I should have cleared that up with Brian, demanded that he accompany her when she brought the engagement ring, rather than agree to seeing her at the same hotel where Brooke and I were spending the weekend."

Brian was Tiffany's boyfriend. We'd had an argument earlier when we brought Tiffany to the hospital, right after I told him about the kissing incident and Tiffany's confession that she still loved me. I could see the anger etched in his face. The reproach. The blame. But now I was glad he knew.

The truth was: Tiffany had been the only one who could get me a customized diamond ring in less than twenty-four hours without Brooke finding out. To my luck, Brian had chosen to believe me. To my misfortune, he didn't let it go easily.

I couldn't blame him.

While I didn't return her affection, Tiffany still felt inclined to love two men. I couldn't imagine the pain Brian was going through. Fuck, I couldn't even imagine why he held on to her. I could only assume that his Irish blood made him loyal to her, like I was to Brooke.

If Brooke loved two men, I had no idea how I'd react. I only knew that I sure as hell would do more than just get into an argument with the guy.

My friends used to call me fearless.

Now my lack of fear had transcended into a lack of tolerance if anyone were to take away what was mine.

"Forget Brian. He'll get over it, dude," Kenny said, breaking through my train of thoughts. "Just as Ti will get over you. It's a matter of time. She already admitted she made a mistake. Something good will come out of this. You'll see."

My brows furrowed.

"Good?" I stared him down. "Are you kidding me? She almost died. Brian blames me. And if it weren't for Tiffany, Brooke and I would be engaged by now, and she'd be in my bed, keeping me warm, if you know what I mean. How can any of this be good?"

Kenny shrugged. "Don't know. But at least you had the guts to tell him."

"I had no choice, really. He would have found out eventually. He runs the gang."

And a huge chunk of NYC, seeing that he had so many connections.

My mood plummeted. "I don't care about his fucking anger. I've experienced it countless times, and it doesn't scare me. It's his unpredictability that bothers me. I wouldn't want his people coming after Brooke," I explained.

Sighing, I raked my hand through my hair as annoyance poured through me fast and furious. When Kenny remained silent, his way to tell me that he agreed with me, I continued, "Frankly, I don't care about Ti right now. I'm more worried about what my girlfriend is up to, and how she got the information about Nate. I don't know what to do. She thinks I'm siding with my brother. Can you believe that?"

I didn't even know why I was revealing my worries to Kenny—thoughts so intimate that I didn't expect my friend to understand.

"Did you at least explain?" Kenny asked quietly, watching me. His voice had dropped to a whisper.

"What?"

"About Tiffany, and your brother."

24

"No." I grimaced. "Not quite."

He straightened and turned to face me. "Definite 'not quite?'"

"I kept it short."

Kenny leaned back, regarding me for a few seconds.

I pressed my lips into a tight line, my heart beating faster as I remembered the morning Brooke confronted me.

"Short?" Kenny's voice was low, but I could still hear the accusation. "How could you keep your explanation about Nate being out of prison short? This is the guy who wanted to kill her."

I gripped the edge of the table and watched my knuckles turn white from the pressure. "You think that this comes easy to me?" I whispered, the words choking me. "Fuck, bro, do you even know how much I hate him?"

The words were sharp and the tone angry.

"Every time I think of Nate, my blood turns to ice," I continued, leaving Kenny no chance to interrupt me. "I don't know how to move forward without this hate consuming me. I don't even know how to sleep at night because my head keeps spinning and thinking of ways to get to him without anyone knowing."

I released my grip on the table and looked up to catch Kenny's expression, while fighting the urge to grab something and destroy it with my bare hands.

Kenny's face remained surprisingly blank.

I moistened my lips, eager to fill the silence with words. "I've never felt so much desire to hurt anyone, not even when I was living on the streets and hated my father's guts for it. But now with Nate out and Brooke anxious, my wish has reached a new peak. I want to kill him—protection witness or not."

I even had the perfect revenge plan. Now, if only I could get Brooke out of NYC.

If only Brooke wasn't so stubborn and unreasonable.

If only we hadn't fought, and my mind could focus on him instead of her.

My hands wiped across my face, as if the motion could get rid of the bitter mark in my soul.

"I get you," Kenny said.

I shook my head slowly. "I don't think you do, because you have no idea what Brooke went through. Or what Nate said to me. It was hard enough to see him there, with that smug smile of his, listening to what he wants to do to her, while keeping up the façade," I said through gritted teeth. "You think he's forgotten? Well, I've got news for you. He told me he dreams of raping Brooke every day. That he is working on having her killed. He described his morbid plans every single time that I visited him, and every time the details became more vivid."

"Why didn't you tell me?" Kenny asked quietly.

Hesitating, I raked my fingers through my hair. "Why?

Because there was no point. It wouldn't have made me feel any better." I looked up at him and caught the dangerous glint in Kenny's eyes. Just like me, he stood by his friends and helped in any way he could, even if that help entailed breaking the law. "Of course, I know he's trying to scare me," I added before Kenny decided to do something stupid. "But if he was speaking the truth, trust me, I'm going to kill him first, before he even catches a glimpse of her."

"Killing him won't make you feel better. I don't have to tell you that," Kenny remarked, his tone betraying that he was lying. He was worried about what I might do to my brother. And rightly so.

"Maybe." I stared him down. "But I owe it to Brooke. To my father, who's still in a coma. I owe it to myself for allowing Nate to fool me the way he did. You can't stop me. Not when he's killed so many people and when I know he'll probably do it again."

Kenny leaned forward, his lips curling into a smile. "Stopping you was never my plan. But I'll gladly join you. You tell me when and where, and I'll be there way before you, getting rid of him once and for all."

"No, I'm doing it." I looked at him hard. "It's my job."

Every day I kept telling myself that I'd get my chance for revenge. I wouldn't let someone else rob me of the chance once the opportunity presented itself.

"Then know I'll have your back." His expression was serious.

For the first time, I felt hopeful.

A mutual understanding passed between us. Of course, Kenny would never let me down. He never did.

"So…how are things between Brooke and you?" he asked carefully.

I stood, taking my time with a reply as I headed for the liquor cabinet. Grabbing two glasses and a bottle, I walked back and poured us some bourbon. I handed Kenny his glass, then dropped on the sofa opposite from him. Ignoring his questioning look, I chinked my glass against his before I took a large gulp. It was only when the alcohol began to course through my veins that I could feel myself relaxing a little.

"I told Brooke it's complicated," I said eventually. "That's all she needs to know right now."

"Did she believe you?" Kenny's tone betrayed his doubt.

"No." I shook my head slowly. "Of course not. She believes I want to kill her to get the fucking Lucazzone estate. Seems like we haven't moved an inch in terms of building trust." I grimaced and drained the glass, then refilled it.

"There's still enough time to tell her, you know. I'm sure she'll understand why you need to get away."

I grimaced again. "Why's everyone pushing me? First

Tiffany, then Brian, and now you. You realize Brooke's pregnant?"

"She's a lot stronger than you give her credit for, bro," Kenny said. "If she knew what was going on, she'd play along."

I stared at him. He obviously knew nothing about Brooke if he believed she'd just let me do my thing without getting involved. "And stress her more, or worse, get her involved while risking her life as well as the life of our baby? Sorry, not happening," I said gravely. "Given her condition, I can't take the risk. Her doctor has been very clear. I don't expect you to understand, but Brooke's condition makes her more susceptible to suffering a miscarriage than other pregnant women. It's not worth it." I didn't need to specify what Brooke's "condition" was. Kenny knew she had been drugged and kicked in the abdomen while pregnant. We still didn't know if the baby had been harmed.

"Right," Kenny said. "So you'd rather have her think you cheated on her?" The disbelief in his tone didn't go unnoticed.

"If that's the way to keep her out of this, then by all means, yes. She's free to believe whatever she wants, even though I didn't cheat, and I told her that countless times. It's her choice whether she wants to believe me or not. It's not like I can force her to trust me with something that she doesn't want to accept."

I paused, leaving the rest unspoken. Thunder echoed somewhere in the background as the sound of rain splattering against the window increased in volume. The image of Brooke all alone popped into my mind, and the fact that we were supposed to be on a plane to Las Vegas, where the danger around us would have been forgotten. At least for a while.

"So, how do you think you'll get her away now?" Kenny asked quietly, sensing the direction of my thoughts.

"Don't you worry. I'll think of something. I'm seeing her tomorrow." I looked at him in silence while taking another swig of the liquid that seemed to burn all the way down my throat. "All that matters is that I take her away from NYC and keep her distracted."

"And if she doesn't want to come or doesn't agree to see you?"

I hesitated. The thought of Brooke not wanting to see me had entered my mind before, but I had pushed it to the back of my mind just as quickly. Every time I imagined her slamming the door in my face, or thought of not touching and kissing her, a dull ache formed in my heart. But then I remembered her words, her willingness to give up on us so easily, and the anger returned.

"No idea," I said grimly. "If she doesn't want to see me, I'll stay away until she's given birth, then I'll try to explain. Maybe once her hormones have settled, she'll see more sense."

Kenny shook his head. "That could take months."

I shrugged. Did I have a choice?

"Well, maybe this will help." He tossed a brown package at me. I caught it before it hit my stomach. I had noticed it before, when he had joined me, but I had paid it no attention...until now.

I frowned. "What is it?"

"Courtesy of Brian."

"Brian?" I looked up from the bundle in my hands, surprised. Remembering my earlier argument with Brian, I pulled a face. Gifts from Brian were never a good thing.

"I don't want it," I said and pushed it back to Kenny. When he didn't grab it, I leaned over to press it back at him, if need be, but Kenny held up a hand.

"He insisted." He cocked his head toward the box. "Come on. Open it."

I eyed him dubiously. "Do you know what's inside?"

"No, but I might have some idea."

It felt light and was perhaps the size of a book. The brown paper was cheap and torn at the edges, as though Brian had used it before. As much as I strained my head to guess what lay hidden underneath, I had no idea. Reluctantly, I started tearing off the wrapping, taking my time.

"Is this some kind of joke?" I picked up the small gun,

my frown intensifying. It was barely bigger than my hand and almost as light as a feather. "Because this sure looks like something a woman would use."

Kenny grinned. "Brian said it's for Brooke."

I met his expression with another frown. "What for? So she can shoot me?"

Kenny let out a snort. "I doubt the bullet could pierce through your chest, dude. You should see how tiny it is. Like a pea." He laughed, which only managed to increase my irritation.

"I'm not worried about my chest," I mumbled. "Knowing Brooke, she'd probably aim for my head if she got her hand on this thing. And since she's never learned to aim, she'd probably end up blowing off my toes—or worse." I didn't need to specify what part of my body I was referring to. "Really, Brian could do a better job giving her a club." I placed the gun back inside the package and handed the box to Kenny.

He shook his head. "Keep it. It's hers. Brian wants you to give it to her, and that's exactly what you'll do...unless you want to piss him off even more than you already have."

My suspicions instantly rose. "Why would he persist? I thought he was mad about Tiffany."

Kenny shrugged. "Maybe he isn't as mad as you thought he'd be."

"He was when I left the hospital." I narrowed my eyes.

32

"What happened?"

"He gave you a gun before," Kenny said.

"That was years ago. Before he found out his girlfriend kissed me."

"He didn't find out. You told him. That's different, isn't it?"

It was my time to shrug. "It's all the same to me. I highly doubt just telling him the truth has turned him grateful." I paused for a moment, pondering what could have caused the gang leader to suddenly warm up to Brooke. I couldn't think of anything.

"He's grateful. That's the real reason?" I prompted.

"He said he owes you."

"Owes me for what?" I met Kenny's eyes, noticing his sudden change in mood. His eyes were lit up, and there was a smile on his lips. It had been three hours since I left the hospital.

Something must have happened in the meantime.

I couldn't imagine what it was, what could have changed Brian's stubborn frame of my mind and his annoyance with me.

"You're keeping something from me," I said matter-of-factly. "Spill it."

He nodded as if he had been waiting for this reaction all along.

"Tiffany's pregnant," Kenny said at last. "They found

out about an hour ago."

For a long moment, I stared at him as the words slowly began to sink in.

Eventually, I leaned back, unsure how to react to the news.

"I thought she couldn't conceive," I said slowly.

"That's what they thought, too." Kenny leaned forward, his voice dropping to a whisper. "But she got pregnant, damaged tubes and all. They call it a miracle. If we hadn't found her, she would have died. So Brian feels like he owes you."

I stared at him.

A child had been Tiffany's dream ever since she lost her first.

It was the source of her problems, the constant battle with depression and alcoholism. Brian always said that if she had another child, it would give her a new purpose, a chance to redeem herself, and the strength to stay sober and recover from her addiction.

"That's...." I trailed off, looking for words. When they failed me, I gave up. "Why didn't you tell me when you arrived?"

"I'm telling you now," Kenny said matter-of-factly. "Besides, the look on your face is too priceless to be missed."

I looked at Brian's package, which had remained

untouched in front of me. Kenny picked up on it and continued, "When he heard the good news, he asked me about Nate, then told me to get the package. He wanted to give it to Brooke a long time ago, but he never had the opportunity. Now, with you two separated and Nate out of prison, he wants you to go after her, sort things out. You know, spend time with her."

"Go after her? Isn't he quite the romantic?" I smiled sarcastically. "Forget roses. I'm sure she'll swoon over a gun. I'm sure she'll want to make up in no time, shooting at the stars and all."

Kenny laughed, his eyes meeting mine. There was a glint in them that I couldn't pinpoint. "Look, he knows that Brooke wants to learn how to shoot. He thinks that with you being good at that sort of stuff, you should teach her, spend some time with her. It would make her feel safe from Nate, and she would have some form of protection. Don't you think she should carry a gun now that she is part of the gang?"

I stared at him as alarm bells began to ring in my mind.

Part of the gang?

When the fuck did that happen?

The last thing I needed was for Brooke to carry a weapon—any weapon—and get into even more trouble than we already were.

I shook my head vehemently. "Not happening."

"I know you like the whole damsel in distress crap, but Brooke needs to be able to defend herself. Brian's words. Not mine," Kenny said. "You can't protect her from everything at all times, dude. However, teaching her to shoot a weapon could bring you just a little bit closer to it. If you don't teach her, then someone else will. If you don't want to, she'll find someone else who'll help teach her to defend herself. Someone who'll get the importance of it. The question is who?"

I stayed silent.

He was right, of course.

While I wanted Brooke to be able to defend herself if she ever found herself in danger again, I also wanted it to be me who protected her and defended her with my life, if need be. That I couldn't now sent a piercing stab through my heart.

"She saw someone today," I said, still staring at Brian's gift.

On impulse, I lifted my phone and checked the screen reluctantly. The app I had installed showed that Brooke hadn't yet left her apartment.

Or at least her phone was still there.

My stomach churned at the thought that she might have outwitted me by leaving her phone at home while going out.

She had done that before.

What if Brooke had discarded it on purpose, knowing I had the tracker installed, and was now getting back at me doing God only knew what? Or worse yet, roaming the streets in spite of the danger she was in, like she had done two days ago.

"I called you because I need a favor. I need you to check this address and find out whatever you can about the person who owns GR Photography." I fished a small piece of paper out of my pocket and handed it to Kenny.

The silence lasted for all of two seconds.

"So you need me to hack into his system." There was no surprise in Kenny's voice. No judgment. His expression barely changed, as if he had been suspecting that I might need him for something like this that all along.

"Yeah. Can you do that?" I asked.

"Easy."

"Good." I eyed the paper again. "All I've found out so far is that his name's Grayson Robert. He owns the building, and from his profile on the web, he seems to work as a photographer, but I'm not sure he's the one Brooke's seeing. His name's linked with far too many people."

"So, you want me to check up on him..." Kenny repeated, glancing at his watch. "At 12.30?" When I looked up, there was a grin on his face.

"Is that going to be a problem?" I grimaced. In the past, Kenny had made fun of my obsession with Brooke at every opportunity. I thought he had grown out of his irritating habit.

Fat chance.

By admitting that it was indeed urgent, I would also admit that I couldn't live without Brooke, which was kind of the truth. But did I want Kenny to know that?

"Just do it," I mumbled. "And be discreet about it."

"Well, then let's go." Kenny reached the door in a few long strides, waiting for me to follow. "The sooner you know what your Juliet is up to, the sooner Romeo will get to rest."

I groaned, irritated at his Shakespeare reference.

Trust Kenny to miss the definition of 'discreet.'

Chapter 2

JETT

KENNY'S ROOM WAS decorated in black, which included the walls, the cupboard, and the curtains. Even the bedspread was a soft shade of licorice. Kenny claimed that the color black helped him focus, pushing aside any form of distraction, which was fundamental in his line of work as a professional hacker. The only vivid splashes were the flickering screens of about fifty computers set up all around his desk on adjustable black shelves and a dangling light bulb in the middle of the ceiling.

The moment Kenny slumped down in his chair, he

propped his legs on the desk, and his good hand glided to a keyboard, his long fingers poised over the keys. And then his furious typing began.

Five minutes passed.

Then ten.

I leaned back on the bed, waiting patiently, even though patience wasn't exactly one of my virtues. In this instance, however, I was glad to let him do the work and wallow in my gloomy thoughts instead.

Eventually, the computer in front of him wired up, and the screen filled with numbers and letters that moved so fast, I didn't even try focusing on them.

I jumped up from the bed and leaned over his shoulder, suddenly nervous, suppressing the urge to pace the room.

What the heck could one find about a person through a computer?

I had listened to Kenny's recounts of his many illegal activities so many times that I had no doubt if there was dirt buried in a yard, Kenny would stumble upon a virtual picture of it.

Kenny always joked that no secret was safe from him. And I believed him. He always knew what he had to do, extracting the most coveted secrets as if they were his own.

That was how we found out that my father had been blackmailed and that he had transferred a large lump of money to save his reputation. If he could find out my father's secrets so easily, what could possibly stop Kenny from discovering something that might just change my life...and not for the better?

What if Brooke had been seeing that Grayson guy for longer than I thought?

What if he was some ex she had failed to mention?

Did I want to know?

I swallowed the thick lump in my throat, and my expression hardened, my resolve strengthening.

"I'm in," Kenny whispered, drawing my attention back to him.

My vision focused on the screen. I expected to see images, videos...anything but a black screen with countless strings of symbols, numbers, and letters.

"Yeah? You might want to translate that," I muttered. Admitting that I had no idea what the heck that was pissed me off.

Kenny chuckled, aware of my incompetence around computers.

"What you see is an indirect access to his main computer's hardware. Logs, passwords, photos, emails, hidden folders...you name it, I have access to all of those now. I can basically monitor his every movement, if you want. Give me the word, and I'll even activate his computer's webcam." Kenny's eyes were gleaming as he shot me a sideways glance, and the enthusiasm in his voice was unmistakable. This was his realm, and he made no secret of it. "I've developed a new program that allows me to track every single letter he types on his computer and even record anything he speaks while he's in the same room. It's still in its beta stage, but it should work, seeing that his firewall is down."

At my silence, he turned to face me, and his brows shot up questioningly.

Thinking he was waiting for some sort of acknowledgment, as usual, I nodded. "That sounds great."

Kenny continued to look at me, his finger hovering over the keyboard, and I realized it wasn't praise he was waiting for.

"What the hell are you waiting for?" I asked.

"This is very personal business, man. You could pay her a visit and ask her if she saw someone today," Kenny said softly. "There would be no need to sneak around and invade her privacy."

He said it as if he hadn't done it countless times before.

As if he weren't a hacker—paid to meddle in people's personal affairs.

Talk about hypocrisy.

"Come on." I laughed and raked a hand through my hair. "Are you lecturing me about privacy now? Really?"

"I'm just saying you might not like what you find out and that it could jeopardize your relationship. Once we're in, it'll be like an addiction and there will be no way back. You can't 'undiscover.' You can't retrace your steps and say you didn't know about it. Eventually, it will spill out in a most unfortunate moment and she'll find out you snooped around."

"So?" I frowned. "I don't have a choice but to find out what she's up to and what kind of person she might be seeing. We're talking about my child and my girlfriend here. It's my responsibility to know who she's dealing with and what kind of person he is."

"You don't know that," Kenny said, shaking his head slowly.

"What?"

"That she's seeing someone."

"Well, I do, but that's not even the point." I let out a deep breath, the lump in my throat constricting.

"How do you know?"

"I talked to her. Besides, I took your advice and had her phone traced. Or how else do you I think I got Grayson's details or found her at the club?" I pressed my lips into a tight line. "Believe it or not, she seems to be enjoying her life. Even if I wanted to confront her, I don't think I'm welcome right now. Can't say that I'm too happy about what we're about to do, but I need to know that the people around her don't mean to hurt her. Now if you could just dive in there, that'd be great."

My tone was decisive, leaving no room for discussion.

Kenny caught on to it and shrugged. "Hey, I'm just trying to make sure you won't have one too many regrets." He turned his back to me, his gaze returning to the screen. "Let's check out his correspondence, documents, and so on. Watch this."

With one click, the screen changed to blue. A few seconds passed in silence, which only managed to increase my nervousness. Eventually, the blue screen changed to a desktop cover. I stared at it in surprise, my words failing me.

It was some sort of plant with human-like roots, its thick body resembling a face.

Kenny let out a laugh. "That shit is sick," he said, pointing his thumb to the picture.

I raised my eyebrows and watched his amusement disappear from his face.

"You like it?" He pointed at Grayson's desktop again.

"It's interesting." As much as I hated the fact that the guy might be trying to date Brooke, I couldn't degrade myself by lying about the fact that I found his strange taste in design at least interesting.

Kenny leaned forward with renewed interest.

"It's a mandrake," I remarked.

"A mandrake?"

"I'm sure you've heard of it." The question was: was

Brooke seeing some sort of hippie, a lover of plants, or a very strange individual?

"You think he's seeing her?" I asked, putting my thoughts and fears into words.

"No idea," Kenny said, oblivious to my distress. "But we could go through his most recent documents, see his past activities, and then we'd know their relationship status."

I grimaced again.

Their relationship status.

The way Kenny said it sounded as though it was a real possibility.

Brooke wasn't like that. At least that was what my gut feeling told me. And yet, did I really know her? The mere thought of Brooke dating this plant guy was crazy. Immediately, a nerve started to throb above my left eye, and my hand instinctively went up to my neck to ease the pressure building inside me. My hands balled into fists.

Kenny turned his head to me, and his grin disappeared as he noticed my grim expression. "I didn't mean..." He sighed, pausing. "Shit, man. All I'm saying is that if he saw Brooke today, he might have mentioned her in an email, in some correspondence. They might be friends, or something like that, or maybe he's just—"

I crossed my arms over my chest, cutting him off. "How about you shut up and see what you can find out?"

"All right, man." Kenny's tone was strained with something. It was certainly not worry or guilt. With annoyance, I realized that his lips were twitching, as though he was trying hard to hide his amusement. "Give me a second."

"You sure it's his computer? It doesn't look professional," I asked to change the subject. "The guy's supposed to be a photographer."

"Yeah, check out his logo, dude," Kenny said, pointing to the blue banner below the huge cover. Right in the middle of the screen, almost undistinguishable and hidden by a plant, was:

GR Photography

It was his.

For a few minutes, Kenny's typing was the only sound in the room. My heart began to thump a bit harder as I noticed the countless files cluttering his main folders.

My eyes came to rest on today's date. Brooke had met up with him. What were the chances he'd be mentioning her to someone else? Probably zero, but I had to know anyway. Fighting the onset of desperation, I leaned over Kenny's shoulder and pointed to the folder.

"Click on this one."

As instructed, he opened it. Instantly, hundreds of

pictures flicked to life, all large. All professional looking. All taking part at some kind of dress-up party.

"It seems to be work-related," Kenny commented, stating the obvious. "I doubt we'll find anything here."

"Go through them," I commanded.

"You sure?"

"Yeah, just to make sure we're not skipping anything."

I didn't know what I expected to find. Maybe just seeing Grayson's models would make me imagine what kind of man he was.

Kenny started to click through one picture after another, opening and closing them all.

"There are a lot of girls in here. Lots of *good-looking* girls," Kenny said, amused. "My best guess is Brooke is friends with one of them. Maybe she can get me the numbers of a few."

I frowned at him for not taking this seriously. "Very funny."

Kenny looked up, casting me a side-glance, and I realized he hadn't been joking.

"What?" he said and shrugged his shoulders. "I'd hook up with them if they were available. I mean, we're talking professional models. I certainly wouldn't say 'no'."

"Aren't you dating Sylvie?"

"She's not the exclusive type."

I frowned. "You made that conclusion based on what?"

Kenny shrugged again and said nothing. I realized it wasn't the time or place to make further comments, so I decided to drop the topic.

As Kenny continued to comb through the pictures, the sour taste in my mouth intensified. My heart raced. My stomach churned as the intensity of my suspicion grew stronger, until a hint of nausea rose in me.

And then, there she was.

"Stop here," I whispered. Kenny's hand hovered in the air, ready to resume.

In front of us was a picture of a woman, half-naked, draped over a chair in a seductive pose, next to two other models. Her hair was tied up in a complicated style, and her face wore so much makeup, other people would have had a hard time recognizing her. But I would recognize her eyes anywhere.

I stared at Brooke's face.

It was her, without a doubt. The same brown eyes. The same high cheekbones.

"I'll be damned," I cursed. "What the fuck was she doing there?"

Her dress was shorter than anything she usually wore and almost transparent.

There was an air of confidence about her, a hint of sexiness—like the one of a stripper ready to glide down a pole, showing off her body in the process. Posing the way she had, she didn't look like the Brooke I had fallen in love with. She looked like a different woman.

Like someone I didn't know at all.

"I don't think she's friends with them," Kenny said by means of resuming our conversation.

"What makes you say that?" I couldn't take my eyes off her.

"Well, for one, she's half-naked," he said. " Maybe she is doing it for fun."

"For fun?" I turned to stare at him.

Kenny shrugged. "Lots of women take pole dancing or stripping lessons. Why not modeling, too?"

Could that be the case? Was Brooke trying to learn to be sexier than she already was?

"Well, I want it deleted," I said.

"Sure." Kenny shrugged and pressed a few buttons. The photo disappeared from the screen. "What about the others?"

I stared at the screen as I felt the pressure in my head increasing. "You think there are others?" I finally asked.

Kenny clicked on a folder, and sure enough, more pictures of Brooke popped up. Anger surged through me as I realized they were far worse than the first one.

The room seemed to be alive with people.

People dressed up.

Men standing next to Brooke, eyeing her.

Men who watched her as though she was some sort of merchandise ready to be bought.

Kenny's suggestion was absurd.

It didn't look like Brooke was posing for fun.

I balled my hands into fists again and took a few deep breaths, even though I could barely contain the need to slam my hand right through the wall. For a few moments, I couldn't say a word, too shocked by the discovery.

"At least it's not porn," Kenny mumbled after a long moment, in what seemed a poor attempt at making me feel better.

I shook my head and grimaced. "No, it's worse than that."

Kenny chuckled nervously. "Well, if Sylvie did this kind of thing, I'd ask her to move in with me. This shit is hot. I'd be proud of her. Come on, we're talking about pin-up girls in lingerie."

"Well, hot shit or not, I want these taken down and deleted for good. Can you do that?" I asked through clenched teeth.

"Should be easy enough, but chances are he has some kind of secure server somewhere where he keeps backup copies. It could take me two days to track it down for you and erase the backup stuff. But if I do it, I'll have to erase them all, and it wouldn't be without leaving a trace."

"Just do it," I said, hopeful until I noticed Kenny's

expression. "What?"

"There's just one problem." Kenny swiveled his chair around and faced me. "He might have sold them. If he's a professional photographer, which I think he is, because he's the owner of the building and he seems to have quite the followership, then there's the possibility that he's already sold at least a few. Maybe he's given away the rights."

I raised my brows, not seeing where the heck he was heading. "So?"

"It would take me days, if not weeks or months, to track down all the digital copies and delete them, with no guarantee that they might not still end up online somewhere. From the look of it, he might have even sold them straight to print."

"How do you know?" I asked.

"Let's just say I've attended this sort of event and ordered the originals." He laughed. "Just not from him. And it wasn't really a transaction in the seller's favor."

I frowned, having no idea what the heck he was talking about. But for once, I had no interest in figuring out Kenny's riddles. "So you're saying it's impossible to get them all and destroy them."

Kenny nodded. "If they're on the web, I'd say it's impossible. And if you're lucky and they're not online, you'd still have to find out who bought copies and what they did with them."

I sighed and began to pace the room. Kenny swiveled around in his chair, his back facing the pictures on the screen. "It's a nice one though. She has great legs. She looks hot. The damage is minimal, if you ask me. It's not really a big deal."

Without thinking, I switched off the screen.

I couldn't bear it. Couldn't bear that she was so readily on display.

Looking so sexy, so different, so confident.

It was as though she was a new woman—one I didn't know. And I didn't like that. I didn't like that someone might have touched her, jerking off to her pictures, doing God knows what else. Demanding that she undress. Maybe inviting her back to his home.

His bed.

"She did nothing wrong, Jett," Kenny said warily.

"I know that. But fuck…" I swallowed hard against the waves of anger rushing through me like hot lava.

"What are you going to do?" Kenny asked after a moment.

"I'm buying the rights to all of them, so I'll be the sole owner, obviously," I said dryly.

"All of them?"

I shot him a sideways glance. "Yes, of course. All of Brooke's photos. Before they end up online. The last thing I want is her half-naked pictures belonging to someone. I can't bear the thought of someone jerking off to her pictures."

Kenny shook his head slowly. "How do you think you'll accomplish that?"

"I'm calling this Grayson guy, you know, talk man to man. Settle it with an amount of money he can't refuse. And if that's not working, I'll make sure he changes his mind. He has to. Everyone has a price. I'll just have to find out what his is. In the meantime, I need you to comb through the web for any copies, leaked or uploaded on purpose, while I try to get the originals."

"What about Brooke?"

I hesitated. "She can't know."

"You'll keep another secret?" Kenny asked.

I stopped my pacing near a couch and plopped down, no longer able to ignore the pounding sensation in my skull. "Just until her pregnancy's over."

Kenny shook his head. "Man, I'm telling you, you're hitting deep water. If you decide not to tell her now, the shit's going to hit the fan eventually. Did it even occur to you that Brooke might not want to stop working for him?"

I leaned forward, resting my elbows on my knees as I observed him, taking in his words. "You think she would continue doing this stuff even though she's pregnant?"

Kenny watched me in silence for a few seconds. Eventually, he resumed the conversation. "Well, I could be wrong, but if she's not doing it for fun, I think she's doing it for the money. You said she had debts. Maybe she thinks she has no choice."

"I'll be her buyer." I stared him down, my grim expression daring him to question my decision.

Kenny shook his head slowly. "Behind her back?"

"Yeah. Well, it wouldn't be the first time." At Kenny's confused look, I added, "The Lucazzone estate. I'm trying to find a buyer. As long as Brooke has connections to the estate she inherited, she won't be safe." I started to pace the room again. "She should have told me if she needed money. I would've helped."

"Maybe she doesn't want you to, considering…"

"Fuck, man, you're not helping," I cut him off, irritated by his need for brutal honesty. "I get it. No need to remind me that she's a proud woman."

"No, what I'm trying to say is that if you had told her earlier, she might have confided in you. Now she doesn't trust you anymore."

I stared him down again, my anger consuming me.

"I gotta go." I turned around and headed for the door, ignoring Kenny's voice calling after me.

"Where are you going?"

I didn't reply as I stepped out the door and walked to the training halls.

I needed time alone.

Time to think.

Time to reconsider my plans.

To admit that I had failed.

Maybe not telling Brooke had been a mistake.

Maybe I should have let her in on some secrets, stopped playing games, given her a little bit of information—enough to make her feel that she knew everything and feared nothing.

Kenny had been right all along.

Brooke needed something—anything.

The problem was I had no idea what I could tell her without making her worried, without risking her health. I had no idea how to repair the damage to our relationship. I had so many secrets. I didn't see how adding one more could cause more damage. If only it weren't exactly the same sentence that pushed me into hot water with her in the first place.

There's still time to tell her.

Kenny's words rang in my head.

But what if he was wrong and it was too late?

What if that Grayson guy had touched her? Made out with her? Fucked her?

The thought made me want to punch someone. It got me furious beyond hell.

Contrary to Brooke's belief, our relationship wasn't over. I refused to lose her. How the fuck couldn't she see that?

As long as I still loved her, which I knew would be forever, or as long as forever existed, I would fight for us.

Or at least until I knew for sure she had stopped loving me.

Stopped wanting me.

Maybe I couldn't force Brooke to give up her new pastime, but I sure could make it clear to her that I'd be the only one who had her pictures.

I might not be able to tame her, but maybe I didn't even need to and surely not by force.

Maybe all she needed was for me to put some distance between us, move away for a while until her bitterness settled a little.

Picking up some punching gloves and peeling off my shirt, I stepped in front of the training mirror, my gaze brushing over the many scars I had acquired in my previous life as a member of a gang. They were ugly, hard, visible reminders of a past I wanted left behind. And yet, as much as they had hurt, compared to our breakup, they seemed barely more than a few scratches gathered along the way. The wound Brooke had created was invisible but more shattering than anything I had ever experienced because it contained a single truth:

She didn't trust me enough.

The knowledge stung, knowing that she never might.

An insurmountable obstacle.

Getting married might be a problem. Because how could she possibly become my wife when she couldn't even entrust her heart to me?

Chapter 3

BROOKE

Present day

I USED TO think love was a lesson to avoid, something to capture and throw away if it so much as glanced in your direction. That was until I met Jett Mayfield.

The man who had changed my life.

The one man who instinctively knew how to mess with my head.

Pressing my hand against my heart, I couldn't help but wonder if my ribs were as bruised as they felt from my heart pounding so hard against them whenever I so much as looked at him. How could it possibly be that just looking at him could break and melt my heart at the same time, and yet being away from him made my heart die?

I had no idea.

All I knew was that loving him was not a choice. I had thought his secrets would crush me, and they had, but so had seeing him renew my faith, making me feel hope again, like a phoenix rising from the ashes.

By telling him everything that had happened over the past three days in my crazy life, I felt like a burden was being washed away. As if sharing pain with him would halve the demons inside me. Or maybe it was his green eyes and the gentleness that resided in his touch that opened my soul to him in the knowledge that it was him who could erase all my pain.

At least two hours passed during which I recalled the past events in minuscule detail: how someone had left me an envelope at the hotel, containing information about Nate's impending release and the secret visits Jett had paid him; how I took a new job, met new friends, went out, and that the next day, one of said new friends, Gina, was found dead. I told him of the detective who paid us a visit, questioning me, and how familiar he seemed, that I was sure I had seen him at the hotel. Eventually, I finished with all the things the detective told me about Jett.

Throughout my monologue, Jett didn't interrupt me once.

Not once did he judge or question me.

He just listened—truly listened, as if it was a peculiar story, something extraordinary, except it wasn't.

It was a story of fear.

A story so frighteningly real it almost felt unreal.

A story I hoped would have a happy ending.

At times, he looked at me with a worried frown—like when I mentioned having found Gina's belongings at his place. At other times, he sat there impassively, even when I expected a reaction—any reaction—like when I told him about the job. Right now, his frown was back in place. I had recounted the story about the detective five times, and each time his worry lines seemed to deepen. His hands were clenched into fists, and his rigid stance became more uncomfortable to watch.

I knew how I sounded.

Like a crazy lunatic.

Fear engulfed me at the thought that he didn't believe me, or worse yet, that he thought I was making up the story, and he didn't have the guts to tell me.

"He really looked and acted like a detective, Jett," I whispered and rubbed my hands together in the hope the knots in my stomach would disappear.

"I believe you, without a single doubt." He intertwined

his fingers with mine, and I let him.

Relief washed over me as his thumb began stroke my skin. For a moment, I stared at his hand, big and strong against mine—until his voice drew me back.

"The guy who interviewed you. What did you say his name was?" he asked, his face turned away from me.

It was his first question, carefully phrased as if he had no idea whether I'd allow him to ask it. I swallowed the lump in my throat as I watched him.

"I think Sparrow. No, wait, that's wrong. It was…" I paused and wet my lips as I racked my brain. "Barrow. Detective Barrow. Why are you asking?"

"I'm trying to figure out why he would meet with you." His gaze remained focused on our hands.

"It wasn't me in particular he wanted to see, Jett. He interviewed everyone. That's why I believed him."

"Are you sure?"

"No." I cast my eyes down, trying to remember. "I was the first one he interviewed, and then I left. I don't know what happened after that. Only that he was interested in you, knew your name, and he showed me pictures."

"And the next day you found my apartment a mess?"

I looked at him. My silence forced his gaze to meet mine. "Not just a mess. It was vandalized, Jett."

He nodded, as if that confirmed his suspicions. "What kind of pictures did he show you of her?"

"Just one. It was a headshot of her dead—in the street. There was blood on her neck. Two dots had been drawn on her face, which I'm sure she didn't have when I last saw her at the club."

My voice was shaking as another cold shudder ran down my spine. His hands left mine. I sensed him moving. When I looked up, I watched him pick up a blanket from a drawer, then walk back to me to wrap it around me.

"Thank you," I mumbled.

Jett sat down next to me, his arm going around me to pull me toward him. Together, we leaned back, my head cradled against his chest.

"I can't believe she's dead," I continued.

I wrapped the blanked tighter around me, as if it could protect me from the memories of my past. Memories that had haunted me for such a long time that, at some point, I had been sure they would stay with me forever.

They had defined me.

My body began to shake uncontrollably. Jett's hand stroked my hand gently, his tenderness calming me.

"You sure she was dead?" he asked.

"Gina?"

"Yes."

His question took me by surprise, but really, it wasn't that unexpected.

My gaze met his green eyes. A few weeks ago, his father

had faked his own death, only to be found alive—until Nate shot him and sent him into a coma from which he hadn't awakened. His father's unpredictable condition haunted and anguished Jett, and I couldn't blame him. Robert Mayfield was a potential witness. His statement could expose all the members of Nate's club—if only he woke up.

"She was dead, Jett," I whispered, unable to stop the sarcasm creeping into my voice. "Dead as in dead. Is that what you want to hear? Gina's eyes were half-open. There was a big gash wound on her neck. It looked pretty real to me. I don't think you can fake that." I choked on the words. "I don't know why anyone would kill her."

"It's okay," he whispered. "If you want to, we can stop talking about it."

"No, it's all right. I want to tell you. Need to tell you. Too much time has passed, too many secrets. I want things to be out in the open and for us to be honest with each other. I don't want to ever get back to that place where we don't talk."

His embrace tightened as his hand brushed my face.

"I don't want that either." His beautiful green eyes carried that gentleness I loved about Jett. It was deep. Real. "Us not talking created barriers. I want you to know I never wanted that."

I propped up on my elbow and turned my body to face him fully. "Are you saying you're sorry?"

His smile was gone, replaced with anguish. "I'm saying I went too far. Yes, I made some stupid mistakes, and not being here when things happened was one of them. If I could change it all, I would in an instant."

Tears stung my eyes.

His words were all I had wanted to hear in the past few days.

"I wish I could change it all, too," I mumbled too low for him to hear. A part of me didn't want to break our moment. But if we didn't get this over and done with, Jett would never know the kind of situation he was in.

I closed my eyes, carefully phrasing my words in my head.

"The other two pictures he showed me were of you, Jett," I started. "One was from the night club where you picked me up. And the second one was taken in a coffee shop two weeks ago and showed you talking with a girl. Her name was Sarah Smith. She was murdered."

I let her name linger in the air. I didn't even know why I had added the last piece of information. Maybe out of hope that the name would trigger something in his mind, but it didn't.

Jett remained awfully quiet. But I knew he was processing the information from the way his jaw muscles seemed to work, rhythmically clenching and unclenching.

"Jett?" I prompted, touching his arm. "Do you know

someone by that name?"

He shook his head slowly, showing that he was listening.

"Sarah Smith." He frowned. "Should I know her from somewhere?" It sounded like a question addressed to himself rather than to me.

I cocked my head, assessing him in thought.

"The picture was taken in a coffee shop two weeks ago," I repeated in case he missed it. "You were talking to her. I don't know what you were talking about, but surely you remember. I mean, it wasn't that long ago. Maybe if you think real hard, it'll come to you."

"What did she look like?"

I shrugged. "Blond bob, very young. Her age wasn't clear from the picture. I'd say eighteen, twenty tops. She was wearing a black cuff bracelet around her wrist and her clothes were dark: fishnet stockings, short black skirt."

He shook his head again, and then his eyes grew hazy as recognition dawned on him. His hand rubbed at his unshaved skin.

My breath hitched in my throat.

"You remember her," I whispered slowly.

It wasn't a question.

It was a fact.

"You said dark? Like a goth?" Absentmindedly, he picked a curl of my hair and wrapped it around his finger, hesitating. His jaw was clenched, his lips tight. "There was this girl with black cuffs and rhinestones, yes. I remember waiting for my order when she approached me."

My heart skipped a beat and blood rushed to my ears. I held my breath as I stared at his face, waiting for him to continue.

It was her.

Jett had met her.

I knew it.

"I don't remember her face, how she looked or anything like that, so I'm not sure I'd recognize her again if she wore different clothes," Jett continued, his voice growing quiet. "But I remember thinking that she was too young."

"How so?"

"She said she was a musician trying to make it big. She told me she was sixteen and sleeping on the couch at her friend's place. She asked me if I wanted to buy a copy of her music because she had no money." He looked at me with a strange glint in his eyes, as though he was trying to convey a certain meaning that he wanted me to understand. "I gave her some cash and told her to go back home to her parents. That they were probably worried about her."

I continued to stare at him, unsure of what to think.

"She was a runaway?" I asked at last.

He nodded. "She gave me a copy. I think I still have it back at the office." He remained silent for a moment. "But I didn't know her, Brooke," Jett whispered. "Not personally. Just as I didn't know your friend Gina. You have to believe me."

He looked so sincere. It felt good to believe him.

I found his hand, and we intertwined our fingers again. "I believe you." I looked at him, smiling, and found myself whispering the same words he spoke earlier. "I believe you, without a single doubt."

For a few minutes, we stared at each other, the silence soothing, and then his expression changed to serious again.

"Brooke, if I remember correctly, I met that girl more than two months ago, maybe at the beginning of September. It definitely wasn't two weeks ago, like the detective claimed."

"Two months?" My eyes widened. "You're saying the detective—or whoever he is—lied about that, too?"

He nodded. "Like with the car."

My heart thumped in my chest so hard I was sure it would jump out from fear. Not from Jett, but from what the situation meant. I didn't know what to think or say. All I knew was that the man had pictures of Jett, and that two girls were dead.

"Did you give him your real name, Brooke?" Jett asked.

"No, I didn't." I wet my lips in thought as new memories invaded my mind. "I couldn't. When I started the job, I gave them my sister's name and our old address, where we used to live. It seemed reasonable at that time, and at some point I regretted it, but now I'm glad I kept my true identity to myself."

Another cold shudder ran through me. I took a deep breath and let it out slowly. "What's so strange is that Gina had two dots painted on her. I thought it might be connected to the poem. You know, the one I told you about."

"Can I see it?"

"I left it at the apartment," I whispered. "I thought there was no need to bring it with me."

"Because you thought it was from me."

I didn't reply, didn't even dare look at him, but I sensed that Jett didn't need my confession.

It was the truth—one I couldn't admit.

Wrapping the blanket around me, I got up. Jett followed instantly. His hand clasped around my shoulder, forcing me to turn around, his eyes searching mine.

"I would never break into your apartment at night, and most certainly not to leave a letter, Brooke. Why didn't you call me?" His voice was soft, gentle, pretty much the opposite of when he was angry.

"I couldn't."

"Why not?" He grabbed my hand and gently pulled me to him. "I thought I'd made myself clear enough. I'll always be here for you."

"I know you said it, but…" I paused, hesitating as I

prepared my words carefully. "I didn't believe it. You were keeping too many secrets. And—" I shrugged, as though it didn't matter, when, in fact, his secrecy had made all the difference.

"And what?" His hand touched my chin, raising it so our eyes connected again, the gentleness of his gesture making my heart pound harder. "What, Brooke?"

I drew a long breath and held it for a moment before letting it out. "When we were on the phone last night, I heard her voice."

I couldn't even say her name. Seeing Jett with Tiffany had broken me to such an extent that even speaking her name, or thinking about her, was like taking a stake and piercing it through my heart.

"Is that what you think happened?" He stared at me, his gaze hard. "That Tiffany stayed over at my place?"

"What else was I to assume? It was late. She had booked a hotel. You met her behind my back. Of course I thought you were with her and that I was interrupting." I couldn't help the bitterness seeping into my voice.

"Brooke." His fingers brushed over my cheekbones, gently forcing me to look into his eyes. "I don't care about anyone but you. I'm not with Tiffany. I don't fuck her. We're friends. Okay? There's nothing going on. And there never will be. What happened between her and me is long over. And she knows it."

"Why should I believe you?" There was no accusation in my voice. Just pure calmness. All the anger was gone, leaving behind acceptance. If he was dating Tiffany, I had simply no other choice but to accept it. I had gone through all the usual stages of grief—breaking up with Jett had been like losing him—and finally made my peace with it.

"Because nothing happened," Jett said, his tone firm and quiet. "I visited her in the hospital. That's why. If you don't believe me, ask Brian where I was. He was standing right next to us when I answered your call in her room."

I stared at him, his words echoing in my head.

"Why is she in the hospital?" I asked quietly.

I wasn't curious.

Far from it.

But Brian's words haunted me. He had said nothing about Tiffany being hurt. Was that another plan of hers to get Jett's attention?

"She had a relapse," Jett explained. "We found her comatose on the hotel floor."

"We?"

"Kenny and I."

My gaze dropped to the floor. I tried to fight it, but guilt consumed me.

All this time, I had drawn the wrong conclusion. While Tiffany was in the hospital, I had wished her bad things because I was under the impression she was the root of our problems. I wasn't supposed to feel pity for her. I wasn't supposed to worry, because she didn't deserve it. But now I felt all those things. It made no sense.

"Is she okay?" I asked.

"She will be."

"I'm sorry," I whispered.

"She brought it on herself."

As he stepped closer, he touched the small of my back. With his free hand, he softly cupped my chin.

"Before you get the next wrong idea about me, let me make one thing clear. I don't really have secrets, Brooke. Okay? I didn't kill Gina. I didn't meet with Tiffany to fuck her." He looked at me, daring me to challenge him. "I don't lie, and I did none of the things you accused me of. And *this* is the truth. The one thing I regret is that I wasn't with you the whole time and that I withheld information I maybe should have shared with you."

I opened my mouth to interrupt him, when he pressed a finger against my lips, signaling me to let him finish. "I should have shared the information that I know I want to spend the rest of my life with you. Or that I love you. Or that if there's something that could risk your life or the safety of our child, I would never take that risk."

His words lingered in the air as he continued to gaze at me, his electrifying green eyes warming my heart and penetrating my soul.

Something passed between us.

Love.

Chemistry.

A spark so strong I could almost feel it in the air.

Those three things I thought I had lost.

"Look, Brooke," he continued. "Everything I do, I do for you. For the both of us. All my life I was taught to fight and conquer, never to show weakness, but it was you who taught me to love and surrender, who put in me the fear that I could lose you, who made me treasure what we have. Not Tiffany. Not my past. You."

He pointed his finger at me. "*You* made me fall in love for the first time and helped me realize that I want to keep our relationship at all costs. That I would protect you…and our baby. Sacrifice everything to keep you by my side."

His words made me listen up. There was the slightest hint of fear in his voice. And something else.

I frowned.

What was he afraid of?

Why was his voice shaking?

Why had Jett felt the need to withhold information from me?

As I scanned his expression, something dawned on me.

"You were keeping things from me to protect me, weren't you? That's why you couldn't tell me."

"Brooke." He took a deep breath. I watched him close

his eyes. It was only when he kept them closed, drawing another long breath, that I grasped something was wrong. That he'd possibly withheld more information than I initially thought.

"There are reasons why I couldn't tell you about Nate," Jett said eventually. "It concerns your pregnancy."

My heart lurched in my chest.

"My pregnancy?" I asked. "What are you talking about?"

He opened his eyes, fear reflecting in his impossibly green gaze.

I shrank back from it. My arms went around my belly, as if they could protect me from whatever he was about to tell me.

"What's so terrible that you can't tell me?"

He sighed again, taking his time to reply. When he finally stirred, the room was quiet.

Too quiet.

"Please, sit." He motioned his hand toward the sofa.

"Just say it." I crossed my arms over my chest, not moving from the spot.

Gazing at him, my whole body tensed. "If you don't say it, I swear I'm going to walk out and never come back. I've had enough of your reticence at the most unfortunate moments. I can't take it anymore."

Jett's shoulders dropped. He looked so miserable, I instantly regretted my words—only they were the truth.

I needed him to open up to me. Preferably before the baby was born, because I knew there would be much more to deal with and talk about in the future.

"I thought I could keep it from you, but it's not possible. Kenny, Brian, they're all right. You have to know it." He stared at me pleadingly.

Pleadingly—for the life of me, I couldn't imagine why.

What was so terrible he couldn't tell me?

"Jett?" I touched his arm. "Tell me. I promise, whatever it is, I won't be mad. I'll understand."

He sighed again, avoiding my scrutiny. When he finally looked at me again, his eyes meeting mine, I knew I had won.

"When we found you, rescued you from your captors, you were in a bad condition. Sam ran some tests. That was when he discovered you had a condition."

I was too shocked to process the meaning of his words.

Sam was Dr. Barn, my obstetrician.

"He said that you mustn't under any circumstances face any more stress. That it could endanger your and our baby's life. When he explained that your condition was linked with life-threatening complications, I made the decision, to keep you out of everything and anything."

I stared at him, taking in his words. "Are you saying I'm sick?"

He shook his head. "Not sick. No."

My ears were ringing, my breath came in short rasps.

"What's my condition?" I asked.

It felt like a disease. Something really bad or even disgusting.

Something that would definitely eat away at my peace of mind.

What was so bad that he couldn't tell me?

"It's a severe form of PE." He looked at me in concern, and my eyes widened.

"Preeclampsia?" I stared at him in shock. I had heard of the condition, but I never thought it would affect me. "But I'm only a few weeks pregnant, not twenty. I'm not overweight. I don't suffer from diabetes. How is that even possible? Maybe Sam's wrong."

"You have a rare form that affects your red blood cells and kidneys," Jett said slowly, letting the words sink in. "So now you know why I didn't tell you about Nate. I didn't want to upset you and risk raising your blood pressure. I know it was a mistake, but I had no choice. There was, simply put, no other option but to keep some things to myself. I thought it made perfect sense."

My throat constricted.

"Oh God. My baby is..." I choked on my voice.

"Fine." He pressed my face against his chest, the gesture surprisingly soothing. "The baby's fine. Don't worry about that."

"Why would you keep something so grave from me?" I hid my face against his chest, unable to stop the fear washing over me, his words lingering at the edge of my perception, but not quite reaching my mind.

"To protect you," he whispered. "That's why I followed you and had your phone tracked. I couldn't risk something happening to you. I thought by staying away and telling you nothing, I could keep you calm and safe, but it didn't work. You drew false conclusions and distanced yourself from me. You went out and got drunk."

A drink that was spiked.

He didn't know that part yet.

It was too much.

Tears started to run down my face, and, at the worst of times, I felt nauseous. My head was spinning. My heart was racing. My fingers started to tremble.

I pushed him away as I stepped aside.

Damn my hormones!

Damn my pregnancy!

Leaning forward, I took deep breaths, but they didn't have the calming effect I had been hoping for.

Jett touched my shoulder. "I'm sorry, Brooke. I wanted what was best for you. I promise our baby's okay. We'll get through this."

I turned around. I didn't know why, but suddenly I was angry and fearful. "How do you know? There's something you don't know, Jett. Something I meant to tell you all along. It's the reason why I'm crying."

His arm froze in mid-air, and the room grew silent again.

"What?" His tone was cautious, wary.

"You were right about one thing."

"Right how?"

I moistened my lips, preparing my words. "There's a reason why I called you a wolf the last time you were at my place." I looked at him, unable to stop the unwanted tear trailing down my cheek. "It wasn't a compliment. I did it because I didn't recognize you."

"I'm afraid I don't understand."

A bitter smile crept to my face, and my heart began to hammer at the memories of that one fateful night—the night Gina died. Taking a deep breath, I struggled to find the right words.

"The night when you picked me up from the club and drove me home, I was high as a kite," I began. "I had hallucinations, and I wasn't even really drunk."

"I still don't understand," Jett said.

"I only had like half a glass. When I told Sylvie about that night, she insisted that I take a test. We found out that my drink had been spiked."

For a few moments, the words hung heavy in the air. When the silence began to feel oppressive, I looked up to

Jett to scan his face.

He looked at me like he had seen a ghost. And then his expression changed into something fierce, destructive even. His fingers curled around my shoulders, as though he was about to shake me to see if I was real.

"What do you mean spiked? Who bought the drink?"

"Gina, the girl who died," I whispered, the nausea inside me growing.

"So you're saying you were high." He sounded incredulous, and I nodded.

"Fuck." He shook his head in disbelief. He looked so worried my heart plummeted.

"At least I didn't drink all of it," I mumbled. He pressed his lips into a thin line, and I continued, "It's possible that the test results were wrong." It was a halfhearted attempt at easing the tension.

"I'm taking you to the hospital."

Before I could stop him, Jett stood and heaved me up.

"Jett." I stood my ground. "What about Gina's things and the cops?"

"What's about them?"

I stared at him. "You're being framed, Jett. If the cops were at your place, chances are they searched it, too. They could be looking for you right now."

"That's not my priority right now, Brooke," he mumbled. "First, I need to see that you're safe and well.

And then we'll figure out the rest."

He tugged at my hand, but I made no attempt to follow his silent command to move.

"What?" he asked.

"At least take another car," I pleaded. "If they're looking for your car, they'll find you."

He stared at me for a few seconds, processing my words.

"Okay. I can do that." He pulled at my hand impatiently. "Come on, Brooke. We have to pay Dr. Barn a visit."

Chapter 4

JETT DIDN'T BOTHER asking Kenny for his car. He grabbed the spare keys on our way out and dangled them from his fingers, shooting me a sideways glance that was supposed to say, "It's okay."

It wasn't okay, obviously, but I had long learned not to argue with him when it came to what was acceptable behavior with his friends.

As far as Jett's friends went, they couldn't be more different from mine. The fact that we were leaving a gang's headquarters was a good indication of that.

As soon as we entered the yellow car, Jett motioned me to buckle up and phoned his physician friend Sam to request his immediate presence. Luckily for us, Dr. Barn was available and agreed to meeting with us in half an hour.

The drive to the hospital was shorter than expected. Maybe because Jett hit the accelerator more often than not, overtaking cars and not stopping at a single stop sign. Several times, my fingers itched to grab hold of the armrest, and I bit my tongue to keep from yelling at him to slow down, but my mouth remained shut.

For one, reasoning with Jett was not only impossible, it was fruitless. And second, his distant, rigid expression showed Jett wasn't in the mood for talking. I could see that he was worried, and in turn, his anxiety rubbed off on me. Shivering, I wrapped my jacket around my body, then folded my hands in my lap, fingers intercrossed so tightly that the white of my knuckles showed beneath the skin. Turning my head to the side window, I closed my eyes to suppress the increasing nausea in the pit of my stomach.

It had been my decision to go clubbing, and as such I carried the responsibility. Whatever happened to my baby would be no one's fault but mine. If only I hadn't gone.

My anxiety reached a new peak the moment Jett pulled the car into the hospital parking area and the tires screeched to a halt. We entered through the main entrance and rode the elevator up to the fourth floor, where Dr. Barn's office was situated.

"I'm scared," I whispered to Jett as we crossed the long

corridor and came to a halt in front of a white door.

For the past few minutes, I had tried to stop the shaking. My stomach was already a hard lump of icy stones, the shaking intensifying the freezing sensation inside me.

"What if something's wrong? I could never forgive myself if the baby—" A tear rolled down my cheek. I couldn't speak the words, the thought too horrible to utter out loud.

Jett turned around to face me, his gaze as dark as I felt inside.

"Don't even think like that." He grabbed my shoulders softly and rubbed my arms in a soothing motion. "You'll be okay. You'll both be. We have to believe that."

"But what if it isn't the truth? I don't want to lose the baby."

He captured my face between his hands, and our eyes met once again. "You won't, because everything will be okay. I know it. If anything had happened, you would already have noticed it."

I nodded and buried my face against his hard chest. But the relentless questions in my mind kept racing through my head.

What if my baby died? Where would that leave us?

My stomach twisted into painful knots.

For the first time in my life, apart from that one moment before I was rescued from my kidnappers, I was truly afraid. It wasn't just about the baby; I was scared that I couldn't take any more worries.

For a few minutes, Jett and I stood there, my body pressed against his, his arms wrapped around me in a tight embrace, while I fought hard to forget reality.

It was only when someone cleared his throat that I stepped back and lifted my head, realizing that, at some point, Sam must have approached and I didn't hear him coming.

The first time Sam Barn and I met, it was after I was rescued by Jett and his gang. Back then, Jett explained that Sam was the only physician he trusted. I could only assume that Sam had played some part in Jett's former life.

"Hi guys," Sam said with a warm, infectious smile. He hadn't changed much in the weeks I hadn't seen him. His blond curls still made him look like an Australian surfer. His black glasses gave him a nerdy look.

"Hey," I murmured.

"She knows," Jett explained as a means of hello.

"You told her about her condition?" Sam's gaze jumped from Jett to me, and then back to him.

Jett nodded. "About an hour ago."

Actually, I knew nothing about my condition except that I had a rare form of preeclampsia that had kicked in too early and was potentially fatal. The first time I read about preeclampsia at all was in a book about pregnancy a few weeks ago, and I thought it was some sort of sexually transmitted diseases.

Come on.

Pre-eclampsia?

It kind of sounded like chlamydia. Whoever stumbled upon it, they couldn't have come up with an uglier word, even if they wanted to.

"It's about time." Sam opened the door and motioned us into his office. "Please follow me."

"How many people know about my condition?" I whispered to Jett as we followed Sam through his office to a back door, which was his private examination room.

"Everyone but Sylvie," Jett said.

I frowned. "Why not Sylvie?"

"You think she can keep a secret from you?" Jett's sarcasm was evident.

I rolled my eyes, then gave a forced shrug. "You'd be surprised."

The truth was Sylvie couldn't keep a secret for the life of her.

Especially not from me.

And particularly not one about me.

***

The examination took over an hour. Jett sat next to me,

holding my hand, throughout the entire session. As soon as we were finished, Sam retrieved a chart to go over the results.

"Brooke." As he addressed me, his eyes became two dark pools of worry. "First and foremost, your baby's healthy. Underdeveloped but healthy. That's the good news."

I gave a loud sigh of relief, until I caught Jett's nervous gaze and the serious expression on his face.

"What do you mean 'underdeveloped'?" Jett asked. He looked anything but pleased. Didn't he hear that the baby was healthy?

"The blood flow through the placenta is diminished, meaning the growth is slower than it should be," Sam explained, unfazed.

Jett frowned—a sure sign that Sam's answer wasn't satisfactory to him.

"It means that the baby might weigh less at delivery," Sam elaborated further. "However, I can assure you it won't be a problem later on. It'll still grow to be a very tall adult."

Sam's lips twitched, and I found myself smiling. Jett barely blinked.

"What about Brooke?" he asked. "You said that was the good news, so I gather you have some bad news for us too."

Sam let out a short, nervous laugh, seemingly used to

Jett's inability to lighten the tension. "If you'll allow me, I'll get to that in a minute." He turned to me. "How are you feeling?"

"Okay, I guess." I shrugged, slightly caught off guard. "Worried but okay."

"Have you had any changes in vision?"

"Changes in vision?"

"Like blurred vision or sensitivity to light. Often accompanied by severe headaches," Sam explained, his hand gesturing slightly as he talked.

"Yeah, I've had those recently. But I've read that migraines often come with pregnancies, so a little nausea and exhaustion is to be expected."

Sam didn't return my "don't worry" smile. Instead, he asked, "Do you feel any pain?"

"Sometimes." I pointed to the area below my ribs. "It comes and goes. Nothing major."

He nodded, as if that confirmed his thoughts. "It's part of your condition. The results have shown that your protein levels are excessively high. Your blood pressure is also too high. I'm afraid you won't have a normal delivery."

"What's that supposed to mean?" Jett asked. His face looked angrier than I thought was humanly possible. Something sparkled in his beautiful green eyes—a dark hint of danger.

"It means that if it gets worse—and I won't lie, it's very

much to be expected—a premature delivery will be the only safe option." Sam's eyes stayed locked on me, avoiding Jett's gaze. "Because your condition is severe and your form of preeclampsia is very rare, I'm afraid we'll have to induce the birth much earlier than planned. Otherwise, it'll progress to eclampsia, resulting in seizures and a coma. We want to avoid that, so I recommend more regular prenatal care check-ups until we can determine the best timing for the delivery."

He paused, hesitating, as though he wanted to say more, but decided against it. "I'm sorry, Brooke. I know this is not what you wanted to hear, but there's nothing we can do. You're lucky that there was no damage to the fetus."

"I understand," I whispered, clutching Jett's hand tighter. "When will I have to deliver?"

"If it progresses like this, I'd say no later than in four months." He smiled sympathetically. "But other than that, the baby's fine, Brooke. As are you. Don't worry too much. I'm going to prescribe you some medication, and recommend that you reduce any form of stress as much as possible. If your condition gets worse, bed rest will be necessary, but it shouldn't come to that. As long as you attend your regular check-ups and don't take part in extreme sports activities, such as car racing"—he pointed to Jett who still didn't crack a smile—"everything will be all right."

My lips twitched. "I think I can do that."

Sam looked at the chart again, and the easy-going smile from before spread across his lips. "Now that this has been cleared up, let's proceed to the next bit of good news. I'd like to use the opportunity to say that we've just received new, top-notch equipment, and I've taken the liberty to screen your blood. Based on the results of the medical procedure, which I cannot stress enough is top-notch and the best in the world, I'm happy to announce that we've found no chromosomal conditions."

Jett opened his mouth, but Sam held up a hand to stop him.

"And we've also found out the gender of your baby." He let the words sink in as he continued to smile at us, clearly enjoying every moment. "Now the question is: do the happy parents want to know now or would they prefer to discover at birth?"

There was a short, stunned silence. "I..." Lost for words, I turned my head to Jett and found him staring at me, as speechless as I was.

Seconds passed with none of us talking. Sam stood.

"If you don't mind, I have to check on one of my other patients. But I'll be back in five. That should give you enough time to come to a decision."

The door closed silently, leaving us alone.

"So, what do you think?" Jett asked.

"I think I'm ready." I tried to hide my smile, with little success. "Do you want to know?" I couldn't help the hint of anxiety creeping into my voice.

"More than anything. It would be great to confirm what I've known all along."

I frowned. "Confirm? Is there something you're not telling me, Jett?"

"I know it's going to be a girl," he said. "I can feel it. I felt it the moment you told me you were pregnant."

I shot him a lazy grin. "Strange to hear it from someone who's not pregnant."

"Are you ready for a bet?"

I gritted my teeth. "A bet on our child's gender? Are you serious?"

Seeing my mortified expression, his smile disappeared. "If you're no longer into our games, we can surprise ourselves at birth."

He sounded hurt—a little reminder of our fight and all the horrible things I had said.

I grabbed his hand and squeezed it. "Jett, I wasn't criticizing our relationship. I'm sorry I called our little games stupid. That's not the way I truly feel about them."

He looked at me for a long time, his green eyes shadowed by his thick black eyelashes reflecting an array of emotions.

Eventually, his naughty self won. I could see it before he

asked, "Are you saying you still want to play?"

I nodded. "Yes, I want to play with you and get played. And everything in between."

"Oh, yeah?" A big smile broke through the dark expression on his face, exposing his perfect teeth and lips so kissable I wanted to taste them right there and then.

"But, Jett, don't you think betting on a child's gender is taking it too far?" I asked.

"Not necessarily. It's a story you won't forget easily, seeing that you'll lose, as usual."

"I don't lose, Jett."

"Sure, woman. Whatever you want to believe is fine by me now. I'll change your mind later, behind closed doors." For a moment, his tone carried that hint of a Southern accent he so desperately tried to get rid of. The Southern accent I had fallen in love with and that always managed to make me tingle down below. With a sexy, devilish glint in his eyes, he held out his hand. "If you win, you can call the shots for one day. Noticed the 'if'?"

Of course I did. He always managed to emphasize it so I wouldn't miss it.

I stared at him, ignoring the pang of heat spreading through my body. Our faces were inches apart now, and the tolerable warmth in my stomach turned into a raging flame between my legs. He looked so sexy, I was ready to do way more than only kiss him.

"And what do you want if you win?" I asked, raising my brows.

"You. One night with me. I guess you're used to that demand by now." His ego was having its big entrance again. I smirked. "But this time, there's more. I want to name our child Treasure."

"Treasure?" I stared at him. He had said it before, but the first time he had mentioned it hadn't sounded so—

Final.

Treasure Mayfield.

Treasure Stewart.

Treasure Stewart Mayfield.

The name sounded perfect. I realized that even if Jett would never want to marry me to turn *us* into the perfect relationship, at least our child would have a perfect name.

"What if it's a boy?" I asked.

"Well, do you want to have a boy?" he counter-asked.

"It doesn't matter. I would love them both equally, obviously," I replied. "I'm just saying, what if it's a boy, Jett? What would you name *him*?"

"I've never thought of that because the possibility never even crossed my mind. To be honest, while I would love both, I'm confident that our first child will be a girl."

My heart fluttered at the way he said first.

First—as if there would never be an only one. There would be more. A few more.

"Why?" I croaked.

He shrugged, and his lips curled up, revealing two perfect strings of sparkling teeth. "I just know, and I hope she'll inherit your stunning lips, because I'm a sucker for those. Like big time." He smiled as his thumb traced the contours of my lips. "And your eyes. Big, brown eyes. Don't get me started on how much I love those."

"That's so shallow." I shook my head, laughing. "If it's a girl, I hope she has your green eyes, not mine, because they're beautiful."

"And you call me shallow? Just saying." He laughed a deep and rich, infectious sound, and for a moment, I was reminded why I loved him so much.

Loved his voice.

Loved his body.

Loved everything about him.

My gaze brushed over his lips, engrossed by the way they moved, rendering me unable to hear a word he was saying. All I could think of was what I wanted to do to him in bed.

"Brooke, are you listening to me?" Jett asked, pulling me out of my reverie.

"Huh?" I blinked. "Yes, obviously."

"No, you weren't."

"I was." I nodded eagerly. His grin turned knowing. "Okay, I wasn't. What were you saying?"

A knock rapped at the door, disrupting our conversation, and I made a mental note to resume the conversation later.

"Am I interrupting?" Sam asked from the doorway, his head barely peeking in, as if Jett and I might be busy undressing or having sex. When Jett motioned him in, Sam entered and closed the door behind him. "So, have you guys decided?"

"We want to know, but before you tell us the gender, do you mind answering one very important question?" Jett paused for effect.

Sam nodded. "Sure. Why not?"

Jett shifted until his knees touched mine. "What about sexual activity? And I'm talking about the whole menu. Is there some kind of rule? Restrictions?"

My head snapped in Jett's direction, and my mouth dropped open.

Holy cow.

Talk about being direct.

"Jett!" I slapped his arm playfully. "You can't ask him about *that*."

"You should encounter no problems in that regard," Sam replied. "Sexual activity is actually very healthy, so I strongly recommend it."

Of course he did. He was a guy after all.

"So, the more the better, right?" Jett nudged my

shoulder, insinuation dripping from his tone.

Earth, please, swallow me whole.

A warm blush crept up my cheeks as I stared at Sam, ignoring the sudden urge to walk out. I stifled the urge. As usual, my treacherous body responded. Feeling Jett next to me, and thinking of our bet, made my heart race, and something warm and fuzzy spilled and traveled through my abdomen.

"At least every day." Sam's lips twitched. "Any other questions?"

Neither of us spoke.

"I'll take it that's a 'no,'" Sam said as he turned to us. "Your little one's a girl."

I stared at him, then at Jett, hope breaking wide open inside me.

"It's a girl," I whispered, my throat choking up.

Sam nodded.

Under Sam's curious and somewhat strange glance, Jett leaned forward, his warm breath tickling my ear. "I can't wait to claim my prize, baby. You better make it good. After days of not having sex, not counting my morning quickie, I want to devour you whole, at least twice."

Chapter 5

AS SOON AS Sam had communicated the results, he cast one more of his strange glances at Jett and me before closing the door behind him and leaving us alone in the room. My cheeks glowed and my heart raced with joy as I turned to Jett, taking in his soft features. He leaned against the wall in a casual stance, his hands buried in his pockets, as he smiled at me, our initial playfulness replaced by seriousness…and astonishment.

Neither of us dared to break the silence, that special moment of ours that belonged to just us.

The moment of beginnings I never thought I'd get to see ever again.

Maybe all the bad things that had happened in our relationship had brought us closer together. They sure had made me appreciate what we had more. Even though the good news was unexpected, more surprising was the fact that Jett wanted to have more than one child with me.

Maybe he even wanted a family and we'd live together.

"So…" I started, unsure but barely able to contain my smile.

"So…" he replied.

"So…" I repeated as I watched him inch closer.

He stopped in front of me, grinning. "So…"

I let out a laugh. "Stop it. If you say 'so' one more time I'll—"

He leaned forward and kissed me on my mouth, cutting off my words. His tongue was warm, welcoming, sending a whiplash of new feelings through me. Something deep inside me roused, and a shudder spread through my body.

I wrapped my arms around him and let him suck my lower lip deeper into his mouth, my heart racing while my knees turned all mushy.

When he pulled back, I almost wanted to hold him, never let him go.

If only I weren't so stunned about the news.

"This is amazing. We're going to have a girl in as little as four months," I whispered.

Even speaking it out aloud felt special.

Having Jett's baby was no longer just a speck of hope. Or just a wish.

We knew for certain now.

A simple truth: Jett and I were going to have a girl.

"The best news in days," he agreed. His voice was soft, full of trepidation as he pulled me up from the chair. "Come on. Get dressed. I'm taking you out."

"Where?" I asked, raising my eyebrows.

"Somewhere special. We need to celebrate, of course. We deserve a real treat. Just the two of us. With no one else around."

"I hope we're not going back to the Trio hotel." The words were out before I could stop them. Gazing up at him, I felt my cheeks blushing. "I mean, it's great. It's just—"

"It was a mistake, Brooke." He looked at me, his handsome face ridden with guilt. "I would never take you there again. Trust me, I learned that lesson the hard way."

His words lingered in the air. I let out the breath I was holding.

"Thank you," I whispered.

"For what?"

I shrugged. "For everything."

"Don't thank me, Brooke. If a guy kissed you like Tiffany did me, trust me, I would have punched the hell out of him." He leaned over, his arm brushing me as he pinned me against the wall. "I'm far more jealous than you are, sweetheart. I won't let anyone touch you. Ever. And if someone actually tried that, I can't guarantee that I wouldn't do things I might come to regret later."

I had no idea what to say. My thoughts scattered, and I swallowed the lump in my throat.

"I'm against any form of violence, you know that," I whispered.

"Me too, but sometimes you have to solve problems fists on."

He retrieved his phone from his pocket, then pointed to the 'NO PHONES. Please take your calls outside' sign on the wall. "I need to make a reservation for us. They're serving coffee and smoothies outside. Can I bring you something on my way back?"

"Coffee would be great. Thanks," I said, squeezing into my jeans.

"All right." Jett closed the curtains to give me privacy. "I'll be right back."

Something in his voice made me look up. Or maybe it was the fact that he didn't kiss me on his way out, which he never missed, even if it was just a five-minute trip. But I didn't press the issue. I finished dressing and grabbed my shoulder bag from a nearby chair to make my way out to the private hospital restroom to apply some lipstick and retouch my makeup. But then I stopped. My hand hovered over the handle as I tuned in to Jett's familiar voice carrying over from outside the door.

"You're sure this isn't a mistake?" Jett asked.

I stared at the door.

Hundreds of thoughts raced through my mind, and once more I was reminded of the strange look Sam had shot Jett before he left. It dawned on me that his look hadn't been meaningless. It was a clue he wanted to speak with him alone. As was Jett's excuse to make a reservation. Maybe not an excuse, but he sure had wanted to leave the room.

I pressed my ear against the door as unease washed over me.

Were they talking about me?

I had to know, so I held my breath and listened.

"I did the blood test twice to check Brooke's story," a male voice said. Even though the words were slightly muffled, I recognized Sam's grave tone. "I can confirm that there were traces of drugs found in her system."

A light pause before Jett's voice cut through the silence. "Drugs? I thought there was just one substance."

Someone, probably Sam, cleared his throat. Then the answer came, "No, we found traces of two."

I stared at the door, suddenly faint. My heart felt as though it might jump out of my chest and hide from me. Someone cursed—I assumed Jett—his voice incoherent.

More out of need than want, my hand grabbed the

handle, and as quietly as I could, I opened the door and peeked out. Jett was standing with Sam at the end of the private hall, a few feet away from me.

Both their backs were turned to me, their body postures rigid, betraying their worry. Engrossed in their conversation as they were, they didn't notice me, and I couldn't blame them. I was as shocked as Jett to hear about the test results.

"Which drugs were found?" Jett asked, his voice clear now that the door was open.

"One is known as a date rape substance," Sam said. "The other was the same high-quality drug Brooke was injected with during her abduction. But in a lower quantity. Whoever tried to drug her wanted to make sure she was unable to defend herself and had no recollection."

My heart skipped a beat. I bit my lip hard until I drew blood.

"They used the same drug?" Jett asked hesitantly.

"I think so, yes." Sam's voice carried over in his usual calm and measured tone, as if he was used to giving people bad news. "I'm sorry. I would even go so far as to say it's identical—the same manufacturer. Again, I can only say she's lucky she didn't drink much of it. The combination of alcohol with twice the amount of the drug previously given to her could have killed her this time. She's lucky you were with her. From what you told me, if Brooke had drunk the rest, she might not be where she is now."

"Fuck." Jett raked a hand through his hair, his shoulders slumped, angry. His hand punched the wall before he let out another set of swear words. I flinched. Sam looked at him, unimpressed.

"How come Brooke's drink was spiked?" Sam asked after a small pause.

"She went out."

"Where?"

"To some place called the Hush Hush club. It's a night club."

"She was at the Hush Hush?" Sam sounded surprised. "Are you serious, man? When did that happen?"

"Recently," Jett said. "Why are you asking?"

"There was an incident there."

My breath stalled. Coldness crept into my bones as I gripped the door harder.

"What incident?" Jett asked, repeating the burning question in my head.

Yes, what incident?

"Haven't you read today's news?"

"No." There was a pause. "Should I have?"

"You tell me." Sam's voice dropped to a whisper, low enough for me to have to strain my ears to make out the words. Holding my breath, I stared at them. I could tell from his body language that it had to be important before he even opened his mouth.

"A dead girl was found there," Sam said. "It's good that Brooke wasn't around when it happened."

My body turned cold, and a shiver ran down my spine.

What girl?

I wished I could walk over and question Sam myself.

"Are you saying a girl was found dead last night?" Jett repeated, the incredulousness replaced with weariness.

"Yes."

"Did she happen to have red hair, and was her name Gina?"

"Not sure about the hair color, but the name's correct." The answer came slower than expected. Sam sent Jett a long look. "So you've heard the news?"

"No."

"If you didn't read or hear the news, how do you know about it?"

Jett took his time with his reply. Eventually, he said, "It's a long story."

"One I should know of?"

"It depends." Jett sighed. I watched him take a deep breath and let it out slowly. "Did the girl die behind the night club?"

I held my breath as I watched Sam, who seemed to study Jett for a moment.

My heart pounded hard as I waited for his reaction, confirmation or denial.

Anything.

My chest started to hurt from all the pressure, but worst of all, my mind was spinning from all the new facts.

Finally, Sam exhaled sharply and shook his head. "No, her body was dumped near the club," he said. "By the time the police arrived, she was long dead."

"How do you know?" Jett asked.

"A friend of mine is the medical examiner who's performing the autopsy on her. He's always short staffed, so he called to ask for help. We talked about an hour ago," Sam explained. He clasped his hands behind his back, his thumbs fiddling. It was the only sign that Sam was nervous.

"What else did he say?" Jett demanded.

"Not much. Only that it'd been a long time since he'd seen a case as bad as hers. She suffered for a few hours before she died."

"Suffered how?"

"Multiple stab wounds."

"Raped?"

"Yes, that too," Sam said. "What I'm telling you is unofficial and confidential information because the autopsy's just begun." Sam waited until Jett nodded his consent before continuing, "According to the news, she was last seen leaving the club with a man Monday at two a.m. My friend put the time of death as three p.m. Her body was dumped out of a car roughly twelve hours later, twenty-four hours after her disappearance."

My heart skipped a beat.

Oh, my god.

I had met the detective at seven p.m. He interrogated me and showed me pictures of Gina while she had been ·lying dead somewhere—still undiscovered.

I clenched my hands into fists as cold shudders rocketed through me.

God only knew what horrible things Gina had suffered in those twenty-four hours.

"Wait a sec," Jett said, mirroring my own thoughts. "Are you saying the girl was abducted, tortured at some place, and was already dead for several hours before her body was dumped at the club?"

Sam nodded. "Yes."

"What the fuck?" Jett's shoulders slumped, and he raked his fingers through his already disheveled hair.

"What's going on?" Sam asked.

"You wouldn't believe me if I told you."

"Try me," Sam said calmly. "Does it involve Brooke?"

"Yeah." Jett nodded, the notion carrying as much graveness as his tone. "And me. I'm getting framed."

"By whom?" Sam asked.

"I don't know."

"How could they possibly link you to this girl's death?"

Jett laughed darkly. "You'd be surprised."

Sam let out a sharp breath. "Jesus, dude. Does Brian know?"

"Not yet. I found out this morning. Brooke told me she was friends with the girl." Jett folded his arms across his chest and leaned against the wall. "Is there a way I can get a hold of the video?"

"We don't have it. It was just mentioned in the news," Sam said. "But it shouldn't be hard to get it. Brian could help out, or do you intend to keep it from him?" The slightest hint of reproach came through in his voice. Apparently, Brian had to be kept updated. That Jett hadn't done so that didn't seem to bode well with Sam.

"I might tell him." Jett drew a long breath. "It'd be interesting to know if any more dead girls were found recently."

The sudden pause signaled they were about to draw their conversation to an end. Afraid that Jett would notice me, I closed the door quietly, but that didn't stop me from cupping my ear to the door again.

For another minute or two, the conversation continued, too muffled to make out more than a fragment. Soon, footsteps thudded down the hall. They seemed to come closer, but I didn't move away. If someone entered, I could always pretend I was on my way out because Jett was taking too long.

"Do you think you can do me a favor?" I heard Jett's

voice again.

"Consider it done."

"I need a copy of the autopsy report."

"What exactly are you looking for?"

"I don't know, maybe the presence of the same drug Brooke had in her system. I want to find out if the girl was drugged," Jett said. "Can you get it?"

"You'll have it by tomorrow."

"I need it today."

"Sure. No problem. I'll call when I have it," Sam replied in the same calm tone. "Anything else I can do for you?"

"As a matter of fact, yes."

The steps came to a halt in front of the door. I expected the door to burst open, but it didn't. Reckoning I had heard enough, I retreated to the examination area and held my breath, waiting for the push of the door handle.

It didn't come.

Waiting and not being able to hear what they were saying felt like an eternity. After a while, a door opened and closed nearby, and the next thing I knew the muffled voices were gone.

Not my thoughts though.

I leaned back, taking deep breaths, unable to shake the nausea building up. My sin felt hot, but inside, a cluster of ice-cold cramps seized my stomach.

Gina had been raped. She had been drugged. And she

suffered.

Just like one of the victims I had met during my captivity—Liz.

My throat burned as various emotions crawled up my spine. I tried to stop the memories flooding my mind, the dark times I had tried to forget but never could. My stomach clenched. I rushed to the bathroom and dropped to my knees just in time, before everything I'd eaten that day came up fast, until I was sure my stomach was empty and there was nothing left inside me.

Shivering, I leaned my throbbing head against the cold surface, praying that the pain would stop.

As I sat there, it occurred to me that Jett would be back soon. He couldn't see me like this, so I got up, sprayed water on my face, and then reapplied my makeup and regarded myself in the mirror.

My skin was unnaturally pale, but it wasn't too bad. I looked good enough on the outside.

I chuckled darkly at the word.

Outside... It sounded like I had two faces. Like there were two sides of me.

A true one that had been hidden far too long, and the one that kept pretending everything was fine when that couldn't be further from the truth. That part of me felt heavy now.

I wished a time would come when I could stop

pretending.

When I moved back into the examination room, Jett hadn't returned yet. At least the nausea had passed. But the fear in my bones persisted as I became aware of three facts:

First, Gina's body hadn't even been dropped off at the club when the detective, or whoever he was, interrogated me.

Second, there was every possibility that the same men who once drugged and abducted me had tried to kidnap me again.

And third, the poem hadn't been a message. It had been a threat.

Someone had every intention of framing Jett for a murder he didn't commit. Someone had orchestrated a great plan, probably plotting it for a long time. Someone might still be after me.

And all this time, I had worried that Jett might be the bad guy when it was someone else.

I swallowed hard, not for the first time wondering if I would ever be safe.

Chapter 6

WHEN JETT FINALLY opened the door, at least fifteen minutes had passed. I was sitting on the examination chair, my feet dangling in the air, my body tense, and my pulse still racing. Forcing a smile to my lips, I cocked my head and looked up at him.

"You didn't have to go through all the trouble to make a reservation, you know," I said nonchalantly. "We could have opted for a quick drive-in."

"Right. What kind of man do you take me for?"

He passed me a cup of coffee. I pretended to take a sip, but all I could focus on was the need to control the rising sense of nausea inside my stomach. Wrapping my cold hands around the steaming cup, I watched him lean against the wall and close his eyes. He stood there for a few long moments, alone with his thoughts. I gave him the privacy because I sensed that he needed it.

When he opened his eyes again, his smile was gone and a flicker of knowledge appeared in them. "You heard us, didn't you?"

It didn't even sound like a question.

I shook my head. "Heard what?"

"It's okay, Brooke. No need to pretend. I knew all along that you would be listening."

His eyes pierced mine, and my breath caught in my throat as my smile died on my lips. There was so much intensity in them my heart skipped a beat. I swallowed the lump in my throat, but all it did was amplify the tension coursing through me. As if sensing my distresses, he nodded knowingly. "So...tell me, how much did you hear?"

Deciding there was no point in lying, I shrugged and carefully placed the coffee cup on the table, afraid the shaking of my limbs might cause me to spill the black liquid.

"Almost everything," I whispered. Unsure if he'd be angry, I added, "I wasn't trying to eavesdrop, really, but you guys weren't exactly quiet."

"I wasn't trying to be." He narrowed his eyes, waiting for me to drop off the hundreds of questions I usually had.

When nothing came, he stepped closer and his fingers curled around my wrists. With a soft pull, he helped me down from the chair and sheltered me in a tight embrace, until I could feel his breath on my face. Sexy, masculine, his green eyes ever so magnetizing. My insides clenched at the anticipation of him kissing me.

"Brooke." He let out a slow breath. "I don't want to keep any more secrets from you. Not again. Not after I almost lost you. This is serious. We have to be honest with each other."

Oh, God.

Those were the words I had been waiting to hear, and for a split second, I imagined a life together without lies, without any more secrets, and a real chance to heal our wounds.

I looked up at him, ready to comment, when I stopped still. His eyes were wide and worried, the usual color of emeralds now foggy and dark. His lips were drawn in a tight line—not at all how I imagined he would be when he spoke those words. I sensed then that more was coming. A scolding, possibly, or maybe...

"Jesus, Brooke." His voice came low, insinuating anger—like a sleeping volcano waiting to erupt. "Do you realize that it could have been you?"

I stared at his beautiful face, now contorted with fear and anger, wondering if we would have another fight so soon after our lovemaking. Did I even have that much energy left? I doubted it.

"Nothing happened. You were there and picked me up," I whispered.

Jett shook his head, grimacing. "I'm not talking about the night you were at that damn club. I'm talking about the guy who left the letter and almost broke into your apartment."

A new shudder ran down my spine.

"Yeah, that was scary." I forced a shrug, banishing the memory of hiding, the strong feeling of being trapped in a room with no way to get help, and feeling guilty when I shouldn't have felt that way. "But nothing happened. I'm still here. It's not even a big deal."

He stared at me. "How can you say it's not a big deal? He could have hurt you and our baby."

"But he didn't." Even to me my reassurance sounded pathetic. Unbelievable.

"No, but he could have, and that's all that matters," he growled. "Brooke, you heard Sam. He said the girl was abducted and tortured. You said that you felt watched. What's to say it wasn't him, the same person who killed Gina? And what's to say he didn't try to get you?"

He was right. The danger had been there all along.

I swallowed, again and again, but the lump in my throat didn't loosen.

The memory of my own abduction brought new and old fears to greater heights.

"You don't have to assume the worst just because you see a few connections," I said more to myself than to him. His brows shot up at my words. "It might have been a joke or...the letter was dropped off at the wrong door." I winced at how unconvinced I sounded.

He shot me a long look.

"Is that what you really believe?" he asked, brows knitted.

I sighed. "No."

"Then what do you think happened? Please enlighten me, because any other explanation than what I've offered you doesn't make sense."

Crossing my arms over my chest, more to stop the shivering than to ward off the cold, I shook my head. Not because I didn't believe he was right, but because I might have been pretty close to the truth before. The mention of tears in the poem, the dots Gina had drawn on her face, were all signs that Jett was right.

Someone was after me.

Jett had mentioned a game before.

"I don't know," I admitted, feeling desperation washing over me again. "It might just be a game like you said, but I'm not sure what game."

Exhaling, I brushed the hem of my shirt then jumped up. I grabbed my bag and fished out my phone.

"What are you doing?" Jett asked slowly, watching me

scroll through my contact list.

"I have to call Thalia," I explained, not bothering to look up. "We didn't really get a chance to talk when we heard the news, but there's a chance her drink was spiked, too."

Jett's fingers enclosed mine, the action stopping me.

I looked up, confused, my glance sweeping from his hand to meet his gaze. "What?"

"I don't want you to contact her," he said calmly. "Or anyone else, for that matter."

I shook my head in confusion and pulled my phone out of his reach. "Why not?"

"Let's just say it's not a good idea."

I drew a long breath and let it out slowly. "Jett, Gina was the one who brought us the drinks. Thalia could tell us if she saw someone with her. She could describe him. She was the last one to see Gina alive." I paused to let my words sink in. When he remained quiet, I said, "If we know what he looks like, we might be able to find out who he is. Thalia could even tell us if the fake detective left after I went home or if anything else suspicious happened."

"No." His voice was hard. Determined. "No. You're not contacting anyone. Sam promised to call as soon as the autopsy report comes in. It will show us if there were any drugs in Gina's body. Until we know for sure what's going on, you can't trust anyone, Brooke. Do you understand?"

He stared at me, his gaze impenetrable, unyielding, yet at the same time pleading. "It's too dangerous."

"But—"

"No, Brooke," Jett cut me off. "If the guy isn't a real detective and he showed you pictures of her body, I have every reason to believe the pictures were provided by the killer, or the guy's the killer."

My jaw dropped in shock, my words failing me. During the interrogation, the detective and I had been sitting close together in the small room. I was hard to grasp the fact that I might have been staring at a killer that whole time. The entire conversation, not just with him but also with Jett, had my head spinning, and for once, I wished I had something stronger than coffee.

A full minute passed.

Then another.

When I found my voice again, I was surprised at how calm my words came.

"You think that guy, who interviewed me, *is* the killer?" I asked.

"I wouldn't rule it out." Jett glanced out the window. "And if he isn't, I'm sure he knows who the killer is."

He turned back to me, and, as if sensing the burning question on my tongue, continued, "It takes at least two people to execute a plan and one person to act as a diversion. So, I'm guessing he and someone else are working with the real killer. The question is who? The fact that Gina brought the drinks could mean she was involved somehow, which is why you can't contact her friends."

I stared at his resolute expression, realizing that Jett was serious. My stomach sunk.

"I can't imagine that Gina was involved," I said. "It's not possible."

"Why not?"

"Simply because"—I shrugged—"it would mean that Thalia's involved, too."

"Well, do you think she might be?"

"Hell, no." I grimaced, mad that he would even suggest something like that. "Her pain looked real, Jett. Just because Gina brought the drinks doesn't mean she was involved."

"Someone spiked them," Jett reminded me.

"But that someone wasn't Gina." My voice rose slightly. "I doubt she wanted to be killed."

His eyebrows shot up. "She still got into the car with a guy and let him drive her some place," Jett said softly. "If she was gay, why would she do that unless she knew him?"

He had a good point.

Gina might have known him. They might have been friends.

Unless...

"Maybe she didn't know what she was doing, Jett," I could hear myself defending her. "Like I didn't know what I was doing when you picked me up that night. She might have been so drugged out of her mind that she just went along, unaware of the danger she was in."

He cocked one eyebrow. "You went home with me because you were attracted to me."

Of course, his ego had to make its entrance at some point.

My cheeks blushed. "Yes. That's true, but still."

"We have to be careful, Brooke. Unless we find real evidence, I won't rule out that your friend's involved, and neither should you. For all we know, they all might be."

"They?" I asked breathlessly. "Who's they?"

"Grayson. Thalia. All your *new* friends," Jett said, oblivious to the storm wreaking havoc inside me. "The fact that you scored the job so fast is kind of unusual, Brooke. How often do you find someone getting a job without needing references, especially with you being pregnant? Thalia basically threw it at you while you ordered coffee."

I stared at him when it hit me.

Jett was thinking I was lured in.

By Thalia.

The idea was so crazy I shook my head vehemently. Thalia had been good to me. Her concerns for me looked real. Even though I hadn't known her for a long time, I was sure she wasn't involved. I couldn't say the same about Jett's brother. The knowledge that Jett didn't even seem to consider other options angered me.

Not once had he mentioned his brother's name, even though I was sure Nate and his people were involved somehow.

"What about Nate?" I asked, regarding him coldly.

It was a simple question, and yet the very mention of his brother's name was enough to change Jett's determined expression to something I had never seen in his face.

Disgust.

Contempt.

Pure hatred.

And then in a split second it was gone—as if it had been a figment of my imagination.

Jett shrugged and buried his hands in his pockets. "What about him?"

"It could be him," I pointed out, unable to keep the angry undertones in my voice in check. "In fact, he's the first one I thought of. Not Thalia, nor Gina, nor my new friends, as you so kindly suggested. If someone's playing a game, then that someone might as well be your brother, not people I just met."

"Nate wasn't out at that time."

"That might be true, but I still wouldn't rule him out, and neither should you," I repeated his words.

Every muscle in his face tensed. "Do I need to remind you that he's under surveillance? He couldn't sneak out, even if he tried to."

"What about an insider, someone passing on messages, or trying to help him?" I continued, not ready to drop the topic. "All he had to do was call in a favor from one of his many connections."

Jett shook his head slowly, his expression getting stonier by the second. "No, it isn't him. Can't be. My brother's not my only enemy, Brooke. If you looked into my past, you'd know that. A lot of people want to harm me."

"Especially those led by your brother," I said dryly, relentless.

"Used to be led, Brooke. Used to. There's a difference." His brusque response stopped me, but only to let me catch my breath.

"Jett," I started again, my patience waning. "While everybody was busy looking for the remaining members, Nate had every opportunity to use a distraction to get what he wants, and yes, I believe that includes framing you."

Why was it so hard for Jett to see that the man he called his brother might be the one who was trying to destroy him? Seconds passed as I glowered at him, unable to stop the frustration gripping me, as Jett remained silent. The whole situation was ridiculous. To protect his brother, he was going too far. It was as though he was in a state of denial.

Oh, my God.

Jett *was* in a state of denial. It was my responsibility as his girlfriend to break down the walls that kept him trapped in blindness.

"Is it just me, or are you trying to protect your brother?" I said casually. "Because it sure feels like it."

"My broth—" He grimaced, his handsome face distorting at once, as if he couldn't even say the word. He exhaled sharply, hands balled into fists as he turned his face back to me, cursing. "Fuck, you think I'm protecting this fuck? I would never do that. I just think..." He ran a hand through his hair, leaving his sentence unfinished.

"Think what?"

He stayed silent. I clasped my hands, waiting patiently for him to explain his perspective so I could understand him. He wet his lips, leaving moisture on them. His posture was rigid, his jaw clenched as he turned his whole body to me, his eyes finally looking up. "I don't think my brother would be stupid enough to do this so soon after his arrest. Not when his trial is still pending, and he knows he'd get life. It'd be too easy and obvious to link him to this."

I stared at him, unsure if I should laugh or be mad at his absurd explanation.

Nate was already facing life behind bars. I doubted he cared much about that little detail.

When I noticed Jett was serious, I shook my head.

"Jett," I started slowly, fighting with myself not to lose

my temper. "Maybe he doesn't care about a few more years in prison or being caught. Maybe easy and obvious *is* the answer. I know you don't want to hear this, and I know you guys grew up together and everything, but please... *please* don't tell me you don't think Nate is involved. It sure looks like it."

"He lost, Brooke." Jett smiled, but his smile didn't reach his eyes. "He has nothing to gain by doing this."

I shook my head again. "See, this is where you're wrong. He has a lot to gain."

"How so?" He frowned. "His account is locked. He's lost his business, and he's betraying the other members by snitching on them. Even if the club continued to grow, and I'm saying 'if', Nate would be replaced as the leader. As things stand now, they'd turn against him if they found out he ratted them out."

I nodded, taking in his reaction. "That might be true. However, you forgot a few things." When Jett frowned, I continued, "He *loves* to kill, but more than that, and you said so yourself, he *loves* to win. Maybe Nate doesn't care that he's being stupid or reckless. Maybe he just wants to destroy your life because he can't bear for you to have it all. All his life you were his competition. That's what you told me, right?" I looked up and found Jett's stance rigid, listening, his face an expressionless mask. "I know it's hard to believe that, but sometimes the most complicated question has the simplest answer. By framing you, he would stop you from acquiring success, from having it all, even if that means destroying your life. ..." I trailed off and stepped back, sort of expecting Jett to be angry, but he wasn't.

I expected him to deny my statements, but he just stood there, looking out the hospital window, his gaze distant, lost in a past he had come to terms with.

"You said I'm forgetting a few things?" he prompted at last, before turning to me. "You only mentioned one."

Towering over me, he looked dangerously handsome. If it weren't for the pain written on his face, I would have kissed him, begged him to take me home so we could celebrate our news instead of obsessing over Nate. Suddenly I wasn't sure if I wanted Jett to hear any more of what I had to say.

I contemplated my next words. Taking my time with a reply, I walked to the window and stopped next to Jett, my gaze fixed on him. His posture was rigid, his jaw still clenched. Anger wafted from him in thick, long waves, but I could feel that his anger wasn't addressed at me. I concluded then that Jett needed the truth spoken aloud as much as I did. Maybe Jett needed to hear me say the words, to have his own fears and doubts mirrored so he could finally acknowledge and come to accept them.

"What most serial killers want: a legacy," I answered.

"Or in Nate's case, a big headline."

His forehead wrinkled, and he opened his mouth to comment.

"No, please listen to me." I held up a hand, silencing him. "Everything Nate's done so far has been for his reputation. Even if he's no longer the leader, like most serial killers, he's immensely proud of his achievements. The headlines, every dead body found—they are trophies. A gain worth far more to him than money or his people. Even if everything's over and destroyed, every member of the club exposed, he'll want everybody to remember him as the leader of that club, and yes, that might just mean having his name splashed across the newspaper. But I don't think that's why he's doing it, Jett." I took a deep, calming breath. "I believe he wants you to become a suspect so that the police start to question the evidence you submitted against him, and possibly consider that you might be involved, too. The following investigation would give him more time, maybe even swing the jury in his favor. Even if you're eventually found as innocent, and it was all a waste of time, it would still mean the news would have traveled worldwide. Your reputation would be shattered. The trial might drag on for months, and if you're not released on bail, you might miss the birth of our daughter." I stared at him, the pain inside me all-consuming. Of course, those were assumptions, but Nate wasn't just anybody. Nate was a schemer. He knew how to plan, implement, and consequently destroy. "If someone's playing us, then it would be Nate, not my new friends, Jett."

The air felt cantankerous. I almost wanted to open my mouth again, when Jett stirred, turning his back to me as he spoke.

"Are you finished?"

His harsh words took me by surprise.

I stepped back, suddenly angry. "You don't believe me?"

Shock crawled up my neck as I watched Jett grab my bag. "No, that's not it. I do believe you. That's the thing. I believe what you say is true." With that, he turned away from me and walked to the door, expecting me to follow after him, which I did.

Chapter 7

THE DRIVE BACK to the gang's headquarters seemed overly long and tiresome, filled with awkward silence and tense vibes that were so unusual in our relationship. Leaning my head against the cold glass, I watched the dark clouds hovering over the skyscrapers.

Soon, very soon, it would be raining again.

Was Jett right in his assumption that my new friends rather than Nate might be involved? It all seemed impossible, almost unbelievable, but how could I know the truth in a world where craziness couldn't be restrained?

The soft pounding in my head increased as I remembered the two bags in my car, and the knowledge that the police had been near Jett's apartment. In spite of Jett's warning, I could barely suppress the urge to call Thalia and finally get answers to the questions burning inside my head.

"What are you thinking about?" Jett's voice jolted me back to reality, his tone sharp, as though sensing my turmoil.

I shrugged, glancing at the busy streets. "Nothing."

"You sure?"

I turned to eye him for a moment. The hard mask he had been wearing since the hospital was still in place. His stance was rigid; his eyes were focused on the road ahead, his grip around the wheel tight, as though he needed to gain control over something—anything. Shivering, I wrapped my arms around myself as I realized that the topic of conversation was dangerously close to returning to his brother. Jett would want to continue our conversation at some point, whether I wanted it or not. Seeing that Jett was already disgruntled, I doubted talking about such a sore point would help ease the tension—and particularly not since Jett seemed convinced that Nate held no power behind bars.

"Yeah." I folded my hands in my lap, fidgeting in my seat. "Nothing at all."

"All right." He let out a loud sigh as his foot hit the accelerator. We sped ahead, overtaking two cars. Ignoring his bad mood, I turned my attention back to the clouds.

This was going to be so difficult.

At least your baby's safe, Stewart. Or is it?

The uncertainty made me shiver again.

I closed my eyes for a moment. It had been a long night and three hard days. A few months ago, back when Jett and I started dating, his fast driving had bothered me. Now I was used to it, even bordering on feeling safe. Maybe it was Jett, his authority and personality, but even when he was angry, I felt protected and sheltered. There was something peculiar about the man next to me, as if the control he exerted over the wheel could be applied to all aspects of my life. Or maybe it was just the hope that the faster we went, the more easily we could escape whoever was trying to destroy us.

Escape whatever had been slowing me down.

Either way, I didn't mind his driving.

I just wanted to erase the bad memories, the bad vibes, all the things that haunted us.

Driving fast, if only to get away from it all, and never look back, felt good.

It was only when Jett slowed down that I forced my eyes open and glanced out the window. I instantly recognized the houses, the familiar street sign, and the bakery.

Whoa!

My body jerked into an upright position the moment

Jett pulled up in front of my apartment.

"What are you doing here?" I asked.

He had claimed it was too dangerous to contact anyone, so I'd assumed we couldn't be seen either.

His answer came fast, unyielding. "I want to see the letter."

I stared at him as he pulled the key from the ignition. "That's not a good idea, Jett." Even as I spoke the words, I knew Jett wouldn't listen to a word I said once he had made up his mind. He never did. He never would.

He leaned over and seized my bag from my lap. In one quick motion, he pulled out the keys to my apartment.

I knew then that the only option was to plea.

Before he could open the door, my fingers clasped around his hand, forcing him to listen. "Wait...please."

"What?" He turned around, mild annoyance written on his face as he eyed my grip around his arm, then moved up to meet my gaze.

"We don't need it, Jett."

He shrugged. "Maybe. But I won't take risks, not in this instance. So, where is it?"

I stared at him until awareness descended on me. He was going to let me wait.

In the car.

All alone while he did the hard work.

Playing the protector, as usual.

I frowned. "Won't you even ask me to come with you?"

"You know that's out of the question."

I let go of his hand and crossed my arms over my chest. "No, waiting here in the car for you is out of the question. You can't leave me behind."

He hesitated for a long moment. When he spoke again, his tone had softened. "Brooke, you were kidnapped on this very street. It's too dangerous. I need you to stay in the car. I promise I'll be back in five. Just tell me where it is."

I shook my head, even though I knew he was right.

Being away from Jett would be hard, even if only for five minutes. But what motivated me to hold my ground was the thought that whoever had left the letter could be up there—waiting to possibly hurt Jett. Losing Jett would be unbearable. I doubted he'd understand if I shared my thoughts with him. Before he could utter another word, I opened the door and ushered out of the car, quickly covering the distance to the entrance, when I realized he had my keys.

Shoot.

Now I was in trouble.

The car door slammed shut.

"Seriously?" Jett's deep voice—now a shade darker—bellowed behind me. I didn't turn around as he joined me in four steps, the sound of his shoes thudding against the wet pavement.

When I turned around, I bumped into Jett's hard chest. I suppressed a laugh.

His peeved expression was almost funny; only, Jett most certainly wasn't seeing the humor.

In my hysteria, I stifled another giggle.

"Did you really think you could outrun me?" he asked, annoyed.

"Jett." Letting out a sigh, I tilted my head back to face him, my smile dying on my lips. "We're in the same boat, in the same mess. You either let me go with you or I'll go alone, but you don't get to tell me what I may or may not do. It's my life. You can't stop me from coming with you."

His eyebrows rose ever so slightly at my reply. "It is still my responsibility to protect you, whether you want it or not."

I rolled my eyes. "If you don't take me with you, I won't tell you where the letter is. And let me tell you, it's stashed away in a hidden and secure place. You'll never find it."

It was a little lie, but he didn't need to know that.

The letter was right out in the open, on the table. Anyone would have found it. But my threat did the trick.

Slowly, Jett's resolution crumbled.

"Besides, those are my keys." I held out my hand and jutted my chin out. "Please."

He sucked in air between his teeth. Eventually, he placed the keys back into my hand. "Fine, but you stay behind me. If somebody's there, you run."

Stay behind him? That I could do.

But run?

Yeah, right. I could easily outrun any pursuer, what with my pregnant belly and all.

"You're absolutely ridiculous," I muttered as I opened the door.

"Can't be careful enough," Jett said, misinterpreting me.

He grabbed my hand and pulled me behind him before he glanced over his shoulder, scanning the now busy streets.

The moment we entered the apartment, I felt something was amiss. Maybe it was the air, or the way everything looked so abandoned. My body tensed, and my heart slammed into my chest. Nothing stirred, and yet it wasn't quiet. The soft hum of the street below could be heard all the way up here.

I cocked my head, continuing to listen for any strange sounds, while Jett checked each room.

When he returned to the hall, his expression seemed more resolute than before.

"Everything's clear," he said. "Where's the letter?"

"In the kitchen. I'll show you." With one last glance at the door, I pushed the dark thoughts to the back of my mind and headed for the adjacent room, Jett following closely behind me. I had barely entered when I stopped short. Slowly, I took a step back, bumping into Jett. I drew a sharp breath to ease the sudden burning in my lungs.

What. The. Hell?

On the table, beckoning to us, was a letter.

Except the envelope wasn't white.

It was bright red, cheerful and promising like a Valentine's Day card.

"It's a good hiding place, I gotta tell you," Jett said. Under any other circumstances, I would have rolled my eyes and slapped his arm, but not today. "It would have taken me days to find it." He stepped forward and reached out to take it before I planted myself in front of him.

"Don't touch it."

He turned to me, frowning. "Why? What's wrong?"

A thin layer of sweat settled across my back. "This isn't it."

Jett's gaze jumped from me to the table, and then back to me, his frown deepening when he caught my expression. "This isn't the letter you told me about?"

"No." I shook my head in disbelief. "I don't think so. Someone was here and replaced it. Maybe I need to see an optometrist, but I'm pretty sure I left a white envelope right here. This one's red, so…"

Before I could finish my thought, Jett sidestepped me and ripped it open, not even bothering to touch it carefully. When he drew out a single sheet of paper—red again—I ran my tongue over my suddenly dry lips.

The last letter had been so creepy. What would the new one say?

I stared at him as he read it, my pulse pounding, uncertainty creeping up on me.

Creasing my forehead, I eyed him nervously.

His shoulders tensed, his grip tightened, as he scanned the text.

"What does it say?" I asked impatiently when he made no move to share his thoughts with me.

Jett ignored me.

I stepped closer and craned my neck to catch a glimpse, but Jett tore the paper out of my line of sight.

"Son of a bitch," he muttered and pushed the sheet back inside the envelope.

"What?" I asked wearily. "What does it say?"

"Nothing worth reading."

My heart began to pound against my chest at his cryptic statement. Jett was trying to hide the torment clearly flashing across his face. Usually, he was a good actor, but this time he seemed to fail miserably. When something affected him, it could only mean the news was bad.

"I know that's not true," I whispered. "Let me see it."

"It doesn't matter," he replied. Ignoring him, I tried to snatch the letter out of his hand, and failed. My hands began to shake, and my legs trembled. Deep down I knew that Jett was trying to protect me again.

Was I ready to read it?

No.

I'd never be.

But I had no choice.

If I didn't look, I would never know, and Jett would never tell me what it said because Jett was too overprotective for his own good. Either that, or he was still having a hard time trusting and sharing his thoughts. I really hoped it was the first, because the last thing I needed was having another surprise just because Jett couldn't open up to me.

"Let me read it. " I held up my hand, motioning for him to hand it over.

"I don't think that's a good idea."

I frowned, waiting, my hand still outstretched. With a sigh, Jett handed me the paper.

I took a seat in a nearby chair, hesitating. When I finally mustered up enough courage, I opened the letter and skimmed the text.

When I see her, I wonder does she still think of me?
Last time, she walked away and I waited for her.
Oh boy, this time there is no stopping.
One bird caged, one free,
But all good things are three.
Fly, birdy, fly.

Tomorrow's soon here.
With your brooken wings under the starry sky
I kiss you good night
For tomorrow is soon here and I'll be there

I read it again and again, while anger, fear, and confusion washed over me in thick cascades.

The poem wasn't just a message.

It was a threat.

In my head, it had become a sick melody that seemed oddly familiar, warning me to run.

I felt like a bird, like when Nate had held me a prisoner. Like Gina must have felt when she was captured. She had died, and there was no doubt that I might be next—or why else would someone spell the word "broken" with two oo's, just like my name? Whoever wrote the poem had done it on purpose. I was sure of that.

I swallowed to get rid of the lump rising in my throat, not for the first time wondering if I would ever feel safe again.

I turned to regard Jett.

He was awfully silent, his gaze avoiding me.

"He used the same words," I said, then went on to recall the night with Jett's brother. "Nate promised that he'd be waiting for me."

Jett's hand encircled mine, and ever so softly, he pulled

the letter out of my tight grip.

"It doesn't matter, Brooke," he whispered, crumpling it into a tight ball. "He can't hurt you. I would never let anyone, anything, come between us. Do you hear me? I won't let anybody hurt you. Before they get to you, they'll have to make it past me."

"I know, but what about *you*?" My gaze met his beautiful green eyes now shadowed with worry. "Your brother hates you. I know he does. He told me you would shoot me and then kill yourself."

"That's ridiculous."

"Not when it was his plan to make it look that way." I pointed to the crumpled paper on the floor. "This is personal, Jett. Things could get a lot worse, and I can't protect you."

"Nothing will happen. I'm strong enough to defend myself," he said. "Come on, baby. You know I would kick his ass. And I have good aim. If he so much as takes a wrong step, he's dead."

I smiled at Jett's bad attempt at infusing humor into the situation, but inside I didn't feel like laughing.

Nate had gone to great lengths to fool his brother. What were the chances he would try again?

Everything spoke for it.

"That's not what I meant." I shook my head, eyes wide, as I struggled for words. "Someone has every intention of framing you for a crime you didn't commit, Jett. Someone orchestrated a good plan, probably plotting for a long time." I pointed at the paper again. "This letter is not a coincidence. It's all part of that plan. Your brother's trying to separate us, take you away from me. I know he wants that, because he tried it once, and he'll do it again."

"I won't let anybody, not even my brother, separate us." Jett seemed unfazed by my words. The fact that he wasn't taking my concerns seriously angered me.

I shook my head again, the desperation in my voice leaving a bitter taste on my lips. "You don't understand. Maybe you won't have a choice."

His eyes narrowed to slits, and his posture stiffened even more—the only sign that he wasn't as confident as he tried to appear. When he spoke again, anger had crept into his tone. "Over my dead body, Brooke. I told you."

"The cops searched your place, Jett." I cleared my voice to stop it from shaking as I remembered the morning but failed miserably. "I took whatever I could, but what if the murder weapon was there and I didn't see it? That could happen, right? What if it's too late, and they're convinced you're guilty? I don't know what I'd do without you."

Jett kneeled and placed his hand at the back of my head, pulling me against his chest. "Baby, stop worrying about me," he said, his tone soothing. "I can take care of myself. I have friends who take care of me. And you. We're not alone in this." He touched my womb, more purposefully than intuitively, reminding me of my condition and the need to stay calm—for our daughter's sake.

"But if there's a trial—" I started again, unable to stop the tear running down my cheek.

"There won't be one." He shook his head vehemently, his determination forcing me to look up, to believe him. "They can accuse me all they want, but they can't prove I'm responsible for the murder. I didn't kill Gina, so whoever's planning this would have to produce real evidence that could hold up in court. As things stand, my team of lawyers would shred their charges to bits."

Emphasis on 'team of lawyers.'

The realization that Jett wasn't just anyone made me feel a bit better.

Jett cupped my face and forced my chin up until I had to face him. "I promise I'll get us out of this fucking mess. I also promise that, if it's his fault, I won't let my brother get away with this."

His voice was composed, eerily so, but his expression made me flinch. He had never looked so serious.

I frowned. "I don't want you to do anything stupid, Jett."

"I won't, " he said. For a second, I felt relieved, until I noticed that his expression carried more determination. His jaw stiffened, and there was no doubt that the anger from before had turned into fury at some point.

When he spoke again, the tone of his voice sent a chill up my spine. "I won't give up, and particularly not when it's about you, Brooke. When it comes down to it, I'll stand and fight. I'll find a way, because there's no way in hell I'll give up my life. And you're my life, Brooke. Whoever's messing with you, I'm going to kill him. I promise I'll make him pay someday."

"No," I whispered. "No. Promise me, Jett, that you won't do anything that could get you in trouble."

He turned away. "I can't," he whispered. "That's the one promise I'll never make to you. I promised myself a long time ago that he'd pay the price. I won't back down on my word."

Chapter 8

BARELY THIRTY MINUTES had passed when we reached the gang's place. As soon as we parked the car in the garage, Jett killed the engine. I expected him to head straight inside, but instead he turned to face me, his hand wrapping around mine, the gesture both determined and strangely imploring, as though he was trying his best to avoid a fight but couldn't shift his position.

"Your keys," he demanded.

I fished them out of my bag again and handed them to him. Our fingers touched, and a spark ran up my arm. Under any other circumstances, I would have welcomed it. Now, with Jett absentminded, it felt like enjoying time with him was too much to ask for. He had read the letter, and his already bad mood had now plummeted to something much worse. Whether it could be attributed to the poem or our earlier conversation about his brother, I couldn't tell, but the fact that he was unreachable remained.

Distant.

Secretive.

Lost in his own world.

I hated when he was like that. His stance reminded me of a statue he might turn into any time.

Or worse yet, he might be hatching a plan without involving me.

"So, what are we going to do?" I asked carefully when he made no move to get out of the car. Our eyes locked ever so shortly, before he turned away to gaze out the window. The garage was empty, the silence oppressing.

"There's this big charity fashion show today," Jett said quietly. "I think we should attend, keep up the appearance, let us be seen, and proceed as if nothing's wrong."

I let the thought sink in for a moment.

Attend a charity event?

I could do that, but what about the cops? Maybe whoever was trying to frame Jett had tipped them off. What if they were looking for him? My pulse spiked as I thought of his apartment and the state I had found it in.

"Is it really a good idea?" I asked.

"Our options are limited."

He was right, of course.

Hiding would only make things worse.

"What about Gina?" I asked casually. "What will we do with her stuff?"

"We'll get rid of it."

My head snapped toward him in shock. "You want to—" I broke off, lost for words.

"We'll burn everything," Jett said coolly.

My jaw dropped open. An icy sensation rose through me.

"Burn the evidence?" I choked on my words, the blood rushing from my veins hard and fast. "I'm not sure that's a good idea, Jett."

"Do you have a better idea?" He cast me a sideways glance as he flipped the keys in his hand. "Because if you do, I'm dying to hear it." His cold response rendered me silent.

Holy cow.

Forget the part about me not wanting him to be angry. His wrath was much better than the calculated and stony air about him.

I bit my lip, my thoughts racing.

Did I have a better idea?

Not really, but burning the only evidence sure didn't sound like something any human in their right mind would do.

"Jett," I said carefully. "Your plan's crazy. It's not just Gina's stuff we're talking about. Whatever's in that bag could be real evidence for whoever killed her. There's a necklace that was soaked in blood. That's hardcore evidence, if you ask me."

He stared at me, taking in my words for a few seconds. "Did you take it?" he asked quietly.

"Huh?" I threw up my hands. "Of course I did.'"

His eyebrows rose in question. "Did you find anything else that was soaked in blood?"

"No." I sighed. "Just the necklace. No sight of the murder weapon. But still. I think we should hide everything until we know for sure what's going on. For all we know, we might need it later, and the actual killer could be brought to justice."

"No."

His harsh tone of voice shocked me. I inhaled a sharp breath, taken aback. "No?"

"No," Jett replied again, his voice colder than before. "I don't see the point in hiding it."

I paused as I considered my next option. "What if we ask Sam to run a few tests and see if something comes up before we do it?"

"Find out what? That it was her blood?" Jett's face remained cold as his next reply slashed at me. "We would be wasting everyone's time because there are not going to be any clues."

"How do you know?" I retorted, suddenly angry.

"I just do." He paused, keeping the rest unsaid. When he spoke again, I felt scolded. "In all seriousness, I don't think we'd discover any fingerprints. If any were left, her stuff would never have been at my place in the first place. Don't you think?"

I shut up, but only for a moment.

"Maybe so, but what if there are?" I leaned forward, suddenly more eager to stand my ground. "Think about it, Jett. What if we'll need it later?"

"Later? As in, if there's a trial?" Jett's face distorted into anger, and my heart gave another almighty thud. "Fuck, Brooke. How often have I told you there won't be one? Anything else is not an option."

I remained silent, struck speechless by his anger. When he resumed the conversation, there was a sudden bitter twist in his voice. "We'll burn everything. Full stop."

"But…" I bit my lip hard.

"If you keep doubting it, by all means ask Sam to test the necklace, but you'll see it's just a waste of time. If the cops come knocking in the meantime, we'll have a problem."

"That's the other thing I wanted to talk to you about. Maybe we should see a lawyer first," I suggested.

"A lawyer? You think a lawyer will help?" He laughed darkly as his eyes met mine. "You're so naïve, girl. An attorney's first priority is to make money out of any case. In my case, that would be representing me as long as possible in a drawn-out murder case that spans months, if not years." He shook his head, his lips tight. "No, we have to destroy it. Burn it and don't involve anyone else. If nothing's found, they can't prove it ever existed. No evidence equals no proof. The last thing my company needs is another big headline or a lawyer who sees an opportunity to supplement his bank account."

He had a good point.

But he was still a dick for calling me 'naïve' and 'girl,' especially in that demeaning tone of his. I was an adult woman expecting her first child. No way would I keep my mouth shut about his attitude.

"No need to be a jerk, Jett. I was just trying to help you," I said and watched him get out of the car. He took his time reaching my side. When he opened my door, an amused expression had lit up his face.

"Did you just call me a 'jerk'?" he asked. His cold tone had softened a little.

"Yeah, I did. So what?" I got out and slammed the door. "Excuse me for saying this, but you can be so narrow-minded at times. Burn the evidence all you want. If you make a mistake, it will be all yours."

As I tried to walk past, he stopped me. I glanced at his hand on my arm and heaved a sigh. "What?"

"Thank you."

His words took me by surprise.

Frowning, I looked all the way up to face him. He let go of my arm.

"Say that again," I said, confused.

"Thank you," he repeated. Slowly but unmistakably, his lips curled into his usual panty-melting smile.

The kind of smile that should have been forbidden.

The kind of smile that turned anger to lust and made me want to do anything for him.

To give in so easily felt wrong, and yet my heart gave a knowing jolt.

Weak, Stewart. Weak. That's how bad you're in love with him.

I crossed my arms over my chest to protect me from his sinful smile and stepped back. "Rein in that ego of yours, Jett. It wasn't a compliment."

"It was to me, coming from a beautiful, stubborn woman with her own mind like you." His grin widened, exposing perfect white teeth.

I stared at him, confused by his sudden change of mood. Barely a minute ago, Jett had been angry, and now, it was as if his irritation had evaporated, which was impossible.

I concluded that his perfect smile could only be forced.

"What?" Jett asked, probably reading the puzzlement

written all over my face. Usually, I was kind of an open book.

I shook my head. "Is this fake?"

"What?" He asked, cocking one sexy eyebrow.

"Your smile."

"This?" He pointed his hand at his lips. "I'll let you decide what to make of it."

Before I knew it, he'd inched closer, and, without warning, he cupped my face in his big hands, his lips crushing mine in a heated kiss.

When his tongue slipped into my mouth, I could have rejoiced, happy to escape our problems for a change, happy to oblige.

His lips were warm, inviting, and yet unexpected. They were like an ambush of the good kind, washing away my annoyance with him. The ice I had felt before crumbled under the weight of heat. His kiss, like lava, burned through my very soul. My arms went around his waist, eager for more.

So, when he stopped, his kiss left behind confusion and emptiness.

"That's not fair." I stared at him, tracing my fingers over my tingling lips. "You kissed me."

"Yeah. I did. So what?" He grinned as he leaned forward, a hand on each side of me, trapping me between his strong, sexy arms and Kenny's car, a mischievous grin on his face. "You don't know how cute you are when you're angry."

I shook my head, suddenly annoyed with his game. "And you don't know how close I am to kicking your ass for being an ass."

"You know what? I would love for you to try that." His eyes twinkled, his voice hoarse. "Wanna see how far that gets you?"

I eyed him, more puzzled than doubtful that he had uttered a threat.

It didn't make any sense.

Was he wearing a mask?

"I don't understand, " I said, deciding that any attempt to figure him out on my own would be a waste of time. "I thought you were angry. You sure looked angry to me."

I sort of expected him to deny it. Instead, he softly cupped my face again, forcing me to meet his gaze. Thinking he was about to kiss me again, I held my breath when he explained, "I was angry, but my anger was never addressed at you, Brooke." He wet his lips, his face tensing abruptly. "I'm angry with my brother for causing trouble when it should be over. I'm angry with myself for putting up with him for so long. I'm angry that we can't enjoy our first pregnancy and what should be a wonderful time, and not being able to spend every fucking minute with you. There are so many hindrances—none of which I can resolve right now. But most of all, I can see that you're scared, and that makes me want to beat up that motherfucker. The fact that I can't right now, that I'm stuck in limbo, makes me want to break a few rules just to get to him and force him to pay the price."

"Jett." I touched his arm, my fingers gently trailing up his hard muscles. "Right now, I'm happy that we're safe. That's all that matters. You and me and our baby. As long as they keep him under surveillance, Nate can't get to us."

"You're right." He cradled me against his chest, his muscles still tense—the only indication that he was in turmoil. "I overreacted. If it makes you feel any better, I'll have Sam test the necklace."

"Jett…" I trailed off, unsure of the right thing to say.

"Don't say anything. Just think about it. I'll leave the decision up to you. After all, like you said, we're in this together, and it was about time you shared my burden, right?"

I grinned at him. "That's right."

We smiled at each other, caught in a moment of closeness that didn't need words and reassurances. Jett's soft lips curled up into another sexy, wicked grin.

"I'm already wondering what would happen if I were to kiss you again. Is that bad?" he murmured.

Oh yes, please.

I eyed him for a moment, his smile igniting sparks of

heat between my legs. Not just between them, but traveling into my core, through my belly—warming my soul and every fiber of my being. My lips twitched, and my insides clenched. Mustering all my self-control, I cocked my head to the side, unable to stop the cocky smile spreading across my lips.

"That depends," I replied cheekily. "Will you stop being a jerk?"

He let out a short laugh. "I can't promise that, girl. Sometimes I swear I was born one. It comes as part of the package."

"Seriously?" I pulled my brows up. "You did it again."

"What?" He spread his hands, palms out, feigning confusion.

"You called me a girl."

"A girl?" he echoed in the same tone.

"Yep, that one."

He let his arms fall to the side. Standing back, he removed his black jacket and dropped it onto the hood. Rolling up his sleeves, he casually leaned against the car. "What's wrong with it?"

"It's presumptuous, offensive, if not annoying, especially when you say it with that attitude of yours. When you're pregnant, you don't want to be called a 'girl.' It just doesn't fit anymore, not when you're about to become a mom."

"Even if you're the *one* girl in the whole world for me,

baby, and I intend to keep it that way?" he whispered quietly.

Holy cow.

Big words.

That was all I could think.

As if sensing my one moment of weakness, the one moment I felt like my whole being was split open, he chuckled—a deep, infectious laugh that would get every woman's panties wet.

"For a jerk, you really know how to charm your way in," I whispered, feeling the blush on my cheeks.

He laughed out loud. "For a woman, you really know how to make me want to be a bigger jerk."

"Are you blaming me?" I asked under my breath.

"Well, ever since meeting you, I've been a different man. Doesn't mean I've turned nice, though." His eyes twinkled with mischief as his hands cupped my ass. "But you're right. Sometimes I'm a jerk. However, the way I see it, it's a good thing."

I scoffed. "How so?"

"Let me think," Jett started, putting on a thoughtful expression. "First, it gives me a reputation for being a hard-ass. No one tries to walk over someone who doesn't take shit from anyone."

"Earns you respect." I nodded.

"That's right, baby."

Which was kind of true. Jett might be a jerk, but what truly earned him respect was the way he was: strong, tall, risky, and way too ruthless—at least according to stories and his reputation.

I opened my mouth, but he held up his hand to silence me. "When it's about you, I really like saying 'sorry'."

Jett almost never said sorry, so his statement made me look up, meeting the devious glint in his eyes.

"Now that's a lie. You don't like saying sorry," I said.

"You're wrong. I do." I stared at him, confused when he continued, "See. It gives me the opportunity to make it up to you. Like, for example, I want to say sorry for the next thing I'm about do."

"About?" I frowned at his insinuation when it hit me. He was about to do something naughty. My lips curled up. "You can't say sorry in advance, Jett. It doesn't work that way."

"Well, trust me, in this one case it does."

"Really?" I narrowed my eyes. "What are you sorry about, then?"

"I'm going to say 'sorry' three times." Biting my lip, I looked away, amused as I let him continue. "Well, let me think. There's one for kissing you before. And there's two for always, and I mean *always*, making you wet."

"I'm not always—" The words died in my throat as I glanced up at him.

Holy cow.

Had he just taken off his shirt?

I had no idea whether to be amazed by his ability to remove a piece of clothing that fast, or by the fact that he was so sexy it literally impaired my breathing.

"That's kind of cheating," I murmured under my breath. "Trying to seduce me like that."

"Or maybe I'm just looking for your opinion. You know, fishing for compliments."

As if he needed my opinion. Or compliments.

Rows and rows of hard muscles adorned his body. And his shoulders, oh my god, they were broad and tanned, inviting me to dig my fingernails into them as we rode the waves of passion. I sucked in my breath as he closed the little distance between us, trapping me between his strong arms again.

"Now, what do you think?" he asked, his voice deep and sexy. "Is my workout any good, or what?"

"Nice try," I said, my gaze fixed on his sculpted chest. Swallowing the lump in my throat, I tried to push aside the dirty thoughts infiltrating my mind.

The picture of trailing my fingers down his pronounced abs; him naked in all his glory, looking too delicious to pass on; him lifting me up until I could wrap my thighs around him, and him plunging deep into me, filling me the way only he knew how.

My stomach knotted deliciously as heat pooled between my legs.

"You should look into hiring a trainer who monitors your training," I added.

His mouth twitched faintly. "And would that happen to be you?"

Damn, my surprise remark just went flying out the window.

"What? No!" I smirked as a blush covered my cheeks. "No, of course not. It's not like I know how to use thumbells and all that."

"I think what you mean are dumbbells." He laughed at my confused expression. "A thumbell is a tiny dumbbell to train your thumbs." He made a flexing motion with his digit before he shrugged casually.

"That's a thing?" I asked.

"Yeah, as odd as it may sound. I hear they use it to train for increased speed when text messaging." He grinned. "But to be honest, I think there are better ways to train your thumb and much…much better ways to use it." My pulse sped up at his insinuation.

I laughed. "I don't think so."

"Well, then let me show you."

He towered over me—close enough for me to touch him, and yet not as close as I wanted him. His gaze pierced through me as he interlaced his fingers with mine and then lifted them to his mouth. My body tensed when his lips brushed over my knuckles, the motion sending an electric shiver through me.

"Look Brooke," he whispered. "There's no cure for confidence. And there's no cure for want. It's perfectly normal for you to want me. And it's perfectly fine for me to be a jerk about it, so I would say let's get used to this weird combo and admit you're wet."

"Oh." I rolled my eyes, even though I knew I couldn't hide how much he turned me on. "At the speed you're going, your confidence will soon grow to the moon and back."

"Is that so?" Still watching me, he kissed the tip of my thumb. His lips were soft as he started to place kisses on my skin—soft at first, then growing firmer—like the pressure inside me.

Holy cow.

If a few innocent kisses could do that to me, what would happen once he really turned on the heat?

I stood still, afraid that if I moved I would surrender. It didn't help though.

He leaned forward to whisper in my ear. "It's not my intention to make you wet. I don't have the kind of power to create a chemical reaction. I don't even know why your body responds the way it does, but it's safe to say that you're into me. There are a hell of a lot of things I can do to help you envision what I have in store for you. But I'll keep quiet and surprise you."

"No, forget the moon," I managed to whisper. "It's way too close to Earth. Take the farthest planet in our solar system. That's how big your ego is."

"Ouch."

In one swift motion, he heaved me up. Before I could figure out what he was doing, he carried me over to his red Ferrari and settled me on the hood.

"What are you doing?" I asked needlessly. Excitement coursed through me when his hand moved up my legs, pushing my thighs apart.

Deep down I knew what he wanted, what he intended to do, because somehow he must have sensed my longing, and now he was going to take care of my needs.

"What does it look like?" He cocked a sexy eyebrow at me as he lifted one of my legs. "Whenever I want something, there is no stopping me. I like the feeling of doing whatever I want with you, because you're mine. Mine to hold. Mine to tease. I own you."

"You don't own me," I protested, feeling the heat spreading across my face, inside my body—thick and hot, coursing through my blood—urging me to confess the effect he had on me.

He lifted my dress slowly.

"Soon. Maybe not now, but I definitely will. Call it my

calling. I know when it's time to fill a longing. And right now, I want to fuck you on my car and see how wet I can get you." He grinned as he brushed a hair strand out of my face. "Miss Stewart, ever since the day I met you, I've made it my resolution to make you *mine*. I want to devour you, to make you want me until you feel that no other man will ever satisfy you. I want you mine with your heart, your soul—with everything you've got."

"Sounds like a devil's plan. Where is the contract, so I can sign up?"

He cocked his head, amusement playing on his lips. "Well, what can I say? You're right. I'm a jerk who takes what he wants, which is why I'm keeping these as a prize." Before I could blink, my panties were gone. He held them up in the air—out of my reach. "Just as I thought."

I blinked once. Twice.

"You're giving them back," I whispered coarsely when he stuffed the flimsy piece of fabric inside his pocket.

"Not happening," he said smugly. "I'm keeping those as proof."

"Proof of what?"

"That it doesn't take much to get you turned on."

"By you," I added.

"By me. That's right, baby." He patted his pocket. "Now, next time, there's no need to play hard to get."

I laughed. "What do you want?"

"You know what I need. What we both need," he said as he scanned me up and down. "It goes both ways. It's a game as old as mankind. We can do it the hard way, or you can surrender."

I ran my tongue over my lips.

There wasn't much sense in lying. Jett was already holding the proof in his pocket. Judging by my desire, I was ready to have him right there and then.

It didn't help that I could smell his manly scent.

Or that he seemed available to the idea.

"All right. You can keep them but under one condition," I said.

His eyebrows rose ever so slightly. "I'm listening."

I took a deep breath. "You'll give me something in return."

He seemed to consider his options for a moment, and then he nodded. "That sounds like a fair deal." He stepped back and unbuttoned his jeans slowly. "You're lucky I'm in a generous mood."

Oh boy!

I stared at him in surprise. "That's the first time I didn't have to ask twice, you know?"

"What can I say? I'm full of surprises." He flashed me another wicked grin, enjoying every moment of his glorious victory.

I peered down at his magnificent erection. He was hard

and beautiful, much like a scepter in a king's hand, and Jett was like a king to me—ruling over my heart and my body. I tried to form a coherent sentence, but all I could think of was him inside me.

"Are you trying to impress me?" I asked nervously. "Because if you are, you're kind of succeeding."

"Kind of? No, baby, I wouldn't say I'm trying to impress you. I'd say I'm dying to fuck you."

Judging by the naughty glint in his eyes and the serious tone in his voice, I should have seen it coming, but it was still a surprise.

His finger curled around the fabric of my top, and he pulled it over my head. I shivered as the cold air hit my naked skin. Slowly, he slid a finger under the strap of my bra and pushed it down my arms, exposing my breasts. With a soft moan, he lowered his mouth and sucked on my nipple, his tongue circling and flicking in equal measures.

My body responded instantly with a fire, welcoming his touch, welcoming him—wanting so much of him that I felt like exploding.

I shifted, suppressing a shudder, when his other hand started to move down my waist and settled between my legs, resting against my wetness.

With a sudden eagerness I had grown to love about him, he heaved me up. A shudder of the good kind traveled through me at the thought of him filling me. Whatever his plans were, I had high hopes for them and couldn't wait for him to get started.

There was no denying.

Jett was my weakness.

This sexy god was my undoing.

He dipped one finger inside me, sending a pulsing sensation to my core.

My head began to spin.

"Wet," he whispered in my ear before kneeling between my parted thighs.

"Is this really a good idea?" I whispered, my gaze scanning the empty garage.

"Since when are you opposed to public sex?" Jett asked, his hot breath tickling my skin. "If it helps, everyone's been instructed not to come down here before five."

His hand moved behind my back, and his tongue slipped into my sex, begging me—no, demanding that I play along. His mouth captured me, his lips firm and yet soft, knowing well what they were doing. My skin tingled. My body trembled. The arousal he had ignited in me returned with full force. Leaning back, I lifted my hips to grant him better access.

"Oh God, Jett," I whispered when he pushed in a second finger.

My words seemed to please him because an instant later his tongue began to flick my clit faster.

I started to tense.

"Don't come." That was all he whispered, stopping. My mouth was still tingling from his kiss, my breathing came ragged, and my body was on fire, shuddering with delight.

"What's wrong?" I asked wearily when he straightened.

"It just hit me." He brushed a stray strand of hair out of my eyes. "I'm addicted to you."

It was my turn to raise my eyebrows. "Is that your third sorry?"

"No." He shook his head. "There's nothing like the feeling of wanting someone so much you have to possess them. I'll do whatever it takes to make you weak for me." The way he emphasized each word made me believe everything he said. I bit my lips as his magnificent erection poked my belly, the motion sending shivers of apprehension through me. As if sensing my need, Jett laughed darkly.

"Now I'm not going to deny it, woman. This is my favorite part," he whispered as his erection began to rub against my pulsing entry. And then, with one determined, sensual stroke, he pushed into me.

My breath hitched as he moved deeper, filling me, stretching me.

My hips began to move, rising to meet his thrusts, opening myself up to the pleasure only he could give me.

"Oh, God," I moaned again as my body began to shake

from the sheer pleasure of being filled. I grabbed the edge of the car's hood, more for support than need. Waves of desire shook me, carrying me to new heights.

With a fast push, he hit the deepest point...and stopped.

My eyes fluttered open, my gaze fighting to see through the hazy curtain before me.

It was then that I realized Jett was going to torture me. He wasn't going to let me come easily.

I winced. Casting my gaze to him, I began to plead because pleading was the only tactic that ever worked on him.

"Jett, please," I whispered. "Don't do this."

He grinned. "Do what?"

"Do I have to spell it out?" I swallowed. "You make me want you."

"Doesn't sound bad to me, considering you're leaning against a very expensive car."

Which so happened to be Kenny's.

"Don't stop, leaving me all frustrated." I sighed again, hating to plead. "Don't be a jerk. You know what I mean."

"I already said sorry for being one."

I grimaced. "You can't say sorry for something you haven't done yet. If you do, you're not really sorry for doing it. It's called being mean."

He let out a sexy laugh. "No, I wouldn't call it mean. Mean is when I do this." He pulled out of me and stepped back, his full erection glistening with my moisture.

I stared at him, disappointed and desolate. And so very empty. At the worst of times, I felt overly sensitive.

Seriously, Stewart! Don't let him get to you.

But it was too late.

I was already too deep in his game.

"Why did you even bother starting?" I jumped down from the hood and pulled up my skirt to cover my nakedness. "This is the last time I let you fuck me."

His hands grabbed mine. With a chuckle, he spun me around until my back was pressed against his hard abs.

"Because I like you wet and bothered, that's why," he whispered, his tongue trailing the contours of my ear.

"You're such a jerk. Like a double jerk. You did it on purpose!" I tried to push myself away from him, but he didn't bulge, his arms pinning me in place.

"That I am." He let out a laugh as he lifted my skirt again. My back pressed against him, I shivered at his touch. I glanced at his hand spreading my legs wide open, spreading the moisture, spreading my desire. I moaned, silently begging him for more, cursing at the way he circled my clit with expert strokes.

Desire started to burn through me again.

"What can I say?" he whispered. "I just love it when you're wet. It makes me feel like you need me."

I shook my head, my body shivering from demand. He

had started a fire he needed to stifle.

How far would I go to satisfy my own needs?

Even though my anger was still bubbling inside, I knew I would willingly surrender.

I always did.

Slowly, I turned to face him. "Well, I do need you."

"Well, I need you, too. Maybe more than I'd ever admit."

Before I could utter another word, his lips crashed down on mine. My pulse raced, and my body trembled as he slowly entered me again. I closed my eyes, enjoying him inside me and his skin against mine until I could feel myself letting go, climaxing with an intensity I thought I'd never know again. Before the last rush of release could leave, Jett came inside me.

Chapter 9

INSPECTING MYSELF IN the mirror in the basement
bathroom, I tied up my hair when I heard footsteps behind
me. I kept my back turned to him but followed his every
move in the reflection of the mirror.

He was dressed in a pair of blue jeans that sat low on his
hips, the fluorescent light accentuating his bare chest and
hard muscles. No matter where he was, Jett always managed
to look like he was ready to pose for a playgirl magazine.

"Hey." He handed me the clean clothes I had left
behind when we had sought safety and shelter with Jett's
former gang. "Thought you might want to put this on. Not
that I don't prefer you naked, but it's getting cold."

His beautiful green eyes shimmered mischievously.

"Thanks." Under his heated gaze, I slipped into the underwear and jeans. We had been dating for a few months, but he was still making me nervous whenever he looked at me. Now that I was pregnant, I could see the changes happening to my body.

If they were so obvious to me, they most certainly were to him, too.

He must have sensed my discomfort, because he stepped behind me and whispered in my ear, wrapping his arms around me, "You're beautiful. And you smell so good." His lips touched my skin gently. "You always do."

"Wait until I reach my second trimester. I'll be as big as a balloon with stretch marks as large as the Grand Canyon."

It was meant to be a joke, if only my tone didn't sound so earnest.

"All the more reason to love you. Every scar, every stretch mark will show the journey we've covered together and remind me where we have been and how much I've loved you along the way. I wouldn't have it any other way," he whispered and turned me around to face him. "Brooke, I very much look forward to that day."

"Quite the gentleman you are. And probably a liar." I slipped on my shirt and turned back to the mirror. My gaze traveled to my toiletries bag. A cold lump settled inside my stomach as I thought of Gina's makeup.

"Anyway, I've decided to burn her things," I said

166

casually as I applied some lipstick. "I don't think we'd find any fingerprints, so let's get rid of the bags, like you wanted."

"Okay."

I met his gaze in the reflection. There was no smile on his lips. No satisfaction in his eyes. "Is that all you're going to say?" I asked.

"What do you want me to say?" he asked.

I shrugged. "How about great? Thanks for going along with my plan."

"I already told you I'm fine with whatever you decide."

I turned around slowly, eyeing him up and down. His eyes remained pinned on me, but his face had turned expressionless. After our previous argument, I thought he'd be pleased that I was agreeing with him. Heck, I would have bet on it.

That he didn't seem to care confused me. His hand was still on my hip as he opened his mouth then closed it again, as if he wanted to say something but decided against it. Eventually, he heaved a sigh, and his shoulders dropped. Leaning against the tiled wall, he seemed tired, as though everything was finally catching up with him.

I narrowed my eyes, suddenly uncomfortable.

Jett was known for his secretiveness and unwillingness to talk, but now he looked uncertain, almost as if he was having second thoughts about burning possible evidence.

"We could still hide it, if you've changed your mind," I said. "Either way, I'd be fine with it. Just let me know what you want."

"Will you forgive me?" His question caught me off guard. His expressionless mask was gone, and in its place, I found something else.

Something I couldn't pinpoint.

Here he was, half-naked, the emotions in his expression exposed, his haunted eyes and perfect features too beautiful for his own good.

I narrowed my eyes, knowing he was done with our previous topic of conversation.

Fuck, I had no idea what the hell he was talking about. But the sudden mood swing sure had me worried.

"What is there to forgive, Jett?" I asked nonchalantly.

"The last few days." He smiled gently. "Some plans didn't go as I imagined."

I let out the breath I didn't know I was holding as I realized Jett was back on memory lane.

"Well, welcome to the club." I laughed. "Nothing ever goes the way I want. It's like a cold or something, except I can't ever seem to get rid of it. Maybe you caught it from me."

He shook his head slowly. "It's not just that. I wanted to call you, to see you, but I thought you needed your space, so I gave it to you."

"Space?" I scoffed and flicked my hand. "I got plenty of space the last few weeks, when you told me you had to work. I don't think there was ever a time when I needed you more than I did in the past few days."

"So did I." With one step, he closed the distance between us until I could feel his breath on my lips. His voice dropped to a whisper as his hand cupped my face. "I still do, Brooke. I just wish..." he trailed off, leaving the rest unspoken.

"What?"

"I wish I hadn't lied."

I shrugged. "You didn't really lie, though, did you? You had your reasons, and like I said, I chose to believe you. And if you want to burn everything, I'm with you." I let the words linger in the air until a thought occurred to me. "Is that the third thing you're sorry for?"

"No." He laughed, and then he fell silent again. "No, it isn't. I'm afraid there's one lie I left out, and that's the one I'm really sorry about. It has nothing to do with Gina."

My smile died on my lips.

He hadn't said that something was bothering him, but I *knew* something was going on because he had that mysterious air about him and he was getting all deep on me.

Something's bothering him, and now he's getting weird about it, Stewart.

If I didn't get him to tell me straight away, he'd shut

down soon, the way he always did. My heart lurched at the sudden realization.

"What is it?" I asked.

He wet his lips carefully, a nervous glint flickering in his eyes. "My jacket. There's something in my pocket you need to see. I don't think you'll like it."

His tone had me so worried my heart gave another jolt.

"Jett?" I prompted.

"I'm sorry. You have to look for yourself."

What now?

My pulsed spiked as I turned on my heels. With quick strides, I reached the garage in no time. I didn't even look to see if Jett was following behind. I had to know what could be so important that Jett would lie and fret about it.

The jacket was still where Jett had left it—on Kenny's car.

Oh. My. God.

How much more could I handle?

"What did you do?" I asked as my fingers slipped into the pocket, afraid of what it might be.

It was hard. And kind of small.

When I pulled it out, I gasped.

It was a black velvet box.

And that could only mean one thing.

"I'm sorry." Those words were the first and last he whispered before the world as I knew it changed.

Chapter 10

ONE OF THE things I never understood was love. That four-letter word that spelled trouble. Could it be that love really existed? That it was so potent, leaving a trail of confusion in its wake by attracting nothing but simple words and actions? Or was it the mind's ability to create something so beautiful and scary that it felt real if we chose to believe in it? Whatever it was, I still had a hard time trusting it, especially when it came down to the sinfully sexy Jett Mayfield.

The man, who had the one and only ability to control my heart and mess with my soul.

The man who had conquered my body and tamed my

heart.

Jett had taught me all there was to know about love, but he'd also made me learn how to curse it when it mattered.

Like now, when I was stuck in between a place where I wanted to believe what I hoped to be true and curse the confusion that had filled my heart.

"Jett." My voice sounded awfully choked as I stared at the box in my hand. "What's this? If this is a prank, I swear I'll kill you."

"It isn't." He stepped behind me, his hot breath tickling my neck. "This is pretty serious, and I wouldn't blame you if you ran away again. "

I turned around, not trusting his words, not trusting his smile, not trusting anything he did or said. His words registered with me, and yet, for some reason, I didn't understand them.

I, Brooke Stewart, didn't understand the situation.

For all I knew, Jett might as well have been speaking a foreign language.

It was that damn box that rendered my brain all mushy.

"Why would I run away?" I asked, cringing inwardly.

I sounded so stupid I could have slapped myself, but honestly, he made no sense.

If only my heart weren't beating faster than a humming bird as I looked up at him.

His handsome face turned to me, his green eyes piercing

my heart, and there was this strange knot in my throat that wouldn't go away.

He grinned. "You'd be surprised with a strong, independent woman like you."

I stared at the box in my hand again. It was light and yet heavy.

Could it be earrings to match my necklace?

I mean, there was no point in getting my hopes up, only to see them dashed again.

"Brooke," he started, "I'm sorry that it couldn't be more special. There are no roses, no candles, no music. Nothing to set the scene, but trust me, I had it all planned back at the hotel, and then you ran away. But now is as good a time as any to ask you..." he trailed off, pausing.

"Ask me what?" I shook my head as I stared at the box, completely flummoxed.

Whether I wanted to wear new stud earrings that evening?

That he had found a good luck charm and didn't know how to return it to its rightful owner? Or whether I minded that he had started collecting cross bugs?

My mind raced through different scenarios, each one more absurd than the last—except for one, and that one couldn't be true.

But if it was?

No way.

I mean, we girls dream. We hope and pine. And that's just part of being stupid and in love. Like the part of believing in unicorns, even though no one's ever seen one, at least not in real life. A marriage proposal was pretty much the same. A fairy tale. Something you wished for.

At least, it seemed like a fairy tale to me, because I, Brooke Stewart, was not getting engaged anytime soon.

"What question, Jett?" I asked, slightly out of breath.

"I think you know, because I've made my feelings about you pretty clear." With a smile, he took the box out of my hand, his fingers lingering ever so shortly on mine. "Don't look at me like that." Jett smiled. "I'm not pranking you, so you can stop shaking your head."

Did I shake my head?

Oh my God, I had.

And then he kneeled.

Oh. My. God.

So did that mean…?

It couldn't be.

And yet, it seemed so very true.

I had hoped for it but never thought it'd happen any time soon.

Jett had been pretty adamant that he'd never marry before he'd dated someone for at least five years, and last time I checked, five years hadn't passed yet. I stared at him in shock, at the box in his hand, at his lost expression, and fought the need to figure out if this was what I thought it was.

"Baby," Jett whispered. "I can be a real jerk when I want something. I can be a real jerk when I fight to keep what belongs to me. Fuck, I can be greedy when I need you, and there's no denying, no reason, no doubt that I need you by my side. Which is why I have one wish. That you stay with me. Forever. Not just today, but until the end of time."

He took a deep breath and let it out slowly. Suddenly, he seemed to grow more nervous. Not nervous, like a student taking a final exam, but more like nervous as in afraid to fail. And he was strangely emotional. I could hear the shaking in his voice.

Pausing, his hand held mine, and he continued to stare at me, his eyes shimmering with what I assumed were tears.

My heart skipped a beat.

He meant it.

"Brooke," he started again, drawing my attention back to his face. "There's a reason why I told you that I was sorry, and there's a reason why I hope that I get a chance to make it up to you for the rest of my life. It's because I can no longer wait to ask you that one question. The one question I hope will change your life. The one I hope won't make you run away." He took a sharp breath. I remained quiet, waiting for him to continue. "You once asked me why I love you, even though you never had to ask. I already told you that you're the only woman who's seen the real me and accepted me for who I am. You're the only woman I want by my side for the rest of my life. The only woman I can imagine myself with. So…will you give me the honor and the joy of being your *husband*?"

With tears in his eyes, he opened the box.

My heart slammed against my chest so hard I feared I might faint on the spot. Lost for words, I stared at him, then at the box.

Inside it was a beautiful diamond ring.

And not just any ring.

Ohmygodohmygodohmygodohmygod.

It was an engagement ring.

He was really going for it.

Jett Mayfield was proposing to me.

I held my breath.

My soul rejoiced, my heart slammed in my chest, and my knees grew weak.

Too many words began to swim inside my brain, and yet my mind was too mushy to grasp any of them.

My vision grew blurry. My fingers brushed over my eyes to check for any invisible tears. Even though I couldn't feel the moisture on my cheeks, it was there.

My tears seemed to pour out of me like a river.

And then he smiled—that beautiful smile I had grown to adore. That beautiful smile that made my heart jump every time he so much as looked at me. For a few seconds, I could feel his emotions, as if our hearts beat as one.

"Yes." I nodded and wrapped my arms around him, my fingers clasping at the back of his nape. "Yes, oh my God. Yes."

He breathed out, relieved. "That's good." He grinned as he gathered me in his arms and spun me around. "I thought I'd have to kidnap you and hold you hostage until you said 'yes'."

Chapter 11

WHILE I WAS sure that Jett wouldn't be opposed to giving me some much-needed privacy, I couldn't tell him how much I needed him to get out so I could engage in some girl chat.

It had taken some convincing for Jett to order more Chinese, but the moment the door closed and I got rid of my new fiancé—God, how much I loved that new word—I phoned my best friend Sylvie.

"You won't believe what just happened," I started as I stared at my new ring, barely able to conceal the excitement that came with being proposed to.

Sylvie *had* to know, or else I would be breaking our

ancient girl's promise to convey the news of being engaged, or else—

Which was why I was now standing in front of the mirror, my heart beating fast at the prospect of telling her.

"Whoa, slow down," Sylvie said, unimpressed by my barely contained excitement. "Does it involve Jett?"

My lips twitched. "Yes. How did you know?"

"Oh, my God. You did not bash his car with a baseball bat, did you?"

"No. Nothing of the sort." I let out a snort. That was exactly the thing Sylvie would want me to do.

"What is it then?" she asked, the confusion obvious in her voice. "And why the hell are you shouting? Did you kill him or something?"

"I'm in the bathroom, and Jett's picking up lunch. Last time I checked, he was very much alive."

"But if you're with him, then...Oh shit! You did not!" She sounded shocked. "You did *not* have sex with him again! Please don't tell me you did."

I groaned. "I did, but before you say anything..."

"That's it. You have to get help," she cut me off. I shook my head. As usual, Sylvie was bossy when it came to Jett, not in the least because she wasn't his biggest fan. "I'm serious. This...this obsession with this guy, it has to stop. I gotta tell you, it's pure madness. And I'm putting it nicely, what with being your friend and all."

I groaned again. "Please listen to me."

"No, I'm not listening to any more of your lame excuses. It's not healthy for you. The first thing you need to do is accept that he's bad, bad news, hot or not."

"No, just listen. He proposed." The words slipped out before I could stop myself. Forgotten was the small fact that Sylvie wasn't up to date. And she most certainly didn't know how much I had wanted Jett to propose.

Silence, then hesitantly, as if she wasn't sure she had heard right, "He did what?"

"Jett and I are engaged." I grinned like an idiot, even though she couldn't see me.

The line went quiet. A minute passed. Then another. The silence grew so heavy I was sure Sylvie had hung up.

"Sylvie? Are you still there?" I asked.

"Yes, I am," she whispered, strangely choked. "I'm just waiting to hear some clapping. You'd tell me if I was being pranked on TV, wouldn't you? Because right now, that's exactly what I think is happening and it's not funny. It's not funny at all."

"Jett and I are back on," I said.

"Like 'back on' back on?" Sylvie's voice was stiff, her tone oozing disbelief. I couldn't blame her. She had no idea at all what was happening. In her mind, Jett had cheated on me. Then, in the span of thirty-six hours, Gina was found dead, a letter was left for me, a nightly visit scared the shit out of me, and yes, Jett and I had reunited. And then he proposed.

I had no doubt that explaining everything on the phone would be too much for someone like her. Knowing Sylvie and her tendency to overanalyze and comment on each situation as if she were Oprah, it would take hours to get her to understand.

Hours I didn't have.

Grabbing a stool from the corner of the bathroom, I sat down. "We want to take our relationship to the next level, you know, start a family."

"But..." As expected, the dreaded words came. "He cheated, Brooke. How could you possibly take him back?"

"Sylvie, I got it all wrong. Tiffany was just jealous." I cringed as I realized how I came across. Defensive. Overprotective. "Jett was planning to propose the whole time and she knew it. That's why she tried to make a pass at him in the hope he wasn't serious about us."

"That's what he told you, huh? That son of a bitch. Of course, he wouldn't let you go without putting up a fight. Of course, he's working on his next lie." A snort echoed down the line before her rant continued, "Honey, you can't believe a word he says. He's trying to get into your panties again. He wasn't the one who dumped you, meaning the loser couldn't take a punch to his ego, so he's spun his story around to suit a purpose. Don't fall for his shit. I bet he didn't even get you a ring."

I sighed, then sighed again.

This was going to be so hard.

Leaning forward, I took a few breaths and slowly counted to three—just as I had learned in therapy after my sister died. This time it didn't help ease the tension inside me.

"I know this is a lot to take in," I said slowly. "It came as a surprise to me, too. Really. But, Sylvie, listen to me." I paused for effect before continuing, more convincingly, "He didn't cheat. He really proposed, and yes, I do believe him. And what the hell! Of course he got me a ring, which, by the way, is the most beautiful I've ever seen." I stared at my hand again. It sparkled so much it could light up a room.

Holy pearls!

The ring was stunning, which could only mean that it must have cost him a fortune.

"Is it even real?" Sylvie asked, doubtful, cutting through my thoughts.

"Wow. I can't even believe you said that." I grimaced, my tone sounding hurt. "Of course it's real. Did you forget the fact that Jett's a billionaire?"

"*Exactly*. He's a billionaire."

"What's that supposed to mean?" I asked indignantly.

"For starters, he might have experience in proposing. I

don't even have to tell you how many women he's fucked."

Disappointed, I let my shoulders drop at the lack of excitement in Sylvie's voice. Why couldn't she be happy for us? I knew my engagement made no sense to her, but just this once, I wanted her to pretend.

Taking a deep breath, I closed my eyes.

"Look. I know you mean well, but my future is with him," I said firmly. "If you both can't get along, then I'm not sure you should come to the wedding. This is about my happiness, Sylvie. I don't get to make a choice, because I love him, and he loves me, and I can't change that, even if that means you won't be invited to be there on our big day."

"You're not joking," Sylvie said matter-of-factly.

"No, I'm not," I whispered.

"So you would choose him over me," she said, hurt. "All the years of friendship, and now you wouldn't invite me to your wedding. Now let me remind you: When he breaks your little heart, I'm the one who'll still be there for you, but if you don't want me at your wedding, then by all means, I'll respect your wishes."

Kill me!

My pulse started to pound against my temples. I so didn't want to fight. Whenever Sylvie and I had an argument, it could take days to resolve it.

I hoped today wasn't one of those days.

Fuck, I hoped it wasn't the day our friendship ended.

On reflex, my chest tightened as fear washed over me. Losing Sylvie would be too hard a blow. She was like the glue that held me together when times were tough.

"Sylvie," I started, my voice shaky. "You're my best friend, my other sister. I never said that I'd choose him over you. Of course, I want you to be there on what will be my most important day. But I can't be in the middle of this. I just can't. Right now, I need you to be there for me and not make things extremely hard by jumping to wrong conclusions and fighting against Jett. There's so much more going on that you don't know about."

"I'm looking out for you, sister." Her voice sounded frosty. "As your friend, it's my responsibility to warn you that he keeps twisting his way into your head with all his lies. What did you expect? That I would close my eyes and lie to your face that he's great when he thinks it's okay to do whatever he pleases behind your back?"

"No...yes, maybe. I don't know." My head was spinning. "He lied to protect me."

There was a short silence. Eventually, Sylvie's voice bounced back, the anger in her tone more palpable than before. "I don't understand. Protect you from what? And what's going on that I don't know about?"

The lump in my throat suddenly increased in size. I closed my eyes for a moment. This was the moment. It was now or never.

"Nate was granted a furlough," I said, trying to sound casual, even though a minuscule part of me shrank at that name.

"Whoa! Stop here! Why would they do that?" She sounded so taken aback, I thought she might pass out from shock. "That's crazy. He's a killer who should be locked up behind bars, not walking around, getting a break."

"He isn't exactly walking around," I explained. "They put him under surveillance so that he could record a few conversations with his ex-associates in return for having his sentence reduced."

"What for?"

"They need more evidence," I muttered.

"That's so fucked up. As if they didn't get enough already. Besides, how can they trust a liar?" Her laugh sounded fake and stopped as abruptly as it started. In the background, I could hear a chair scraping across the hardwood floor. Then Sylvie sighed.

For a second, I imagined her, her hand clutching her phone, everything else forgotten. My previous words were still ringing in my ears. Sure, what I had said was harsh, but I had spoken the truth.

"Hold on. I need a drink to digest this. All of it." The line went quiet for a while. That was exactly what I had expected Sylvie to say after hearing the news. Leaning my head against the wall, I imagined Sylvie rummaging in our small kitchen for a bottle of anything, until I realized that she wasn't and couldn't be at the apartment.

"You have a bottle in your office?" I asked incredulously when she was back on.

She let out a forced laugh. "Are you kidding me? How else would I survive in this poorly paid job? But seriously, everyone has a secret stash somewhere." In the background, I could hear a bottle unscrewing and liquid pouring into a glass.

"I hate fighting with you," Sylvie said and took a sip.

"I don't want to fight either," I admitted, strangely emotional.

It was true.

"Good. I mean, it would be stupid to risk our friendship over some—" she stopped abruptly.

I frowned.

Over some guy? Over something else?

The silence grew worse. For some reason, I could sense that Sylvie was fighting with herself.

"You said Nate would be getting a reduced sentence," she started. "How many years are we talking about?"

"I don't know," I said honestly. "I hope not too many, but Nate's looking at life anyway, so it won't really make a difference. That's what Jett said."

"That's what he said, huh?" Her voice sounded stiff, but

at least she had calmed down. I could only guess it was the alcohol now flowing through her system.

A good old glass of wine had probably saved me from the lion's jaw.

"Yeah."

Tense silence ensued.

Stretching out my legs, I waited for her reply—for anything that would break the awkward moment. When nothing came, I closed my eyes. With each passing second, I was getting closer to the moment of truth.

"Just say it," I whispered, feeling every muscle in my body tense.

"Look, if you want to get married, I'll support you. Fuck, I'll tolerate Jett, but don't expect me to love him or anything. You can't expect me to understand why he couldn't tell you about Nate. It's not like it's not a big deal, because it is, and we all know that. But it's not exactly like he couldn't tell you. And please correct me if I'm wrong."

Clutching my phone to my ear, I stared at the wall. I could imagine Sylvie, her fake reading glasses on her nose, a drink in her hand, as she waited for my response, her face scrunched up, thinking she had it all figured out. It was now up to me to be honest about everything.

Set things straight.

My heart stuttered, but she had to know.

"My doctor told him not to," I whispered at last. "Jett

didn't tell me things because of my condition."

"What...wait, what condition?" Sylvie said. "Oh, my God. You're scaring me right now. What condition? Are you sick or something?"

"No, I'm not sick. It's just that..." I trailed off, considering how to explain.

"Don't even think about lying. If you don't tell me, I'll phone Jett and ask him myself."

I brushed a hand over my womb.

"Well, according to the doctors, I have a severe and rare form of preeclampsia, which is often associated with first-time pregnancies," I explained, trying to sound casual. "It could put my life in danger and all that, but I think they're all exaggerating a bit. It had Jett worried, though, which is why he kept things from me. To be honest, I feel fine. I'm happy. I'm engaged. So there's no need to overreact," I added before Sylvie felt the need to jump into a taxi and start cocooning me until the day my daughter was born.

"I'm such a bitch," Sylvie said slowly. "I assumed the worst."

"You weren't the only one," I retorted as I thought back to my confrontation with Jett. I wanted to say more, but her sudden spluttering, then choking and coughing, stopped me short.

"Are you all right?" I asked, worried when her cough worsened.

"Sorry. My drink went down the wrong pipe." She cleared her throat. When she spoke again, her tone was oddly tearful. "Look, I didn't mean what I said before. You know, about Jett. I had no idea he was trying to protect you."

I shrugged and squeezed nonchalance into my voice— enough to fool her. "It's all right."

"No, I'm really sorry." She sounded so emotional my heart gave a jolt. "I shouldn't have acted the way I did. It was harsh and uncalled for. Not only toward Jett, but toward you as well. I'd never...like ever... have forgiven myself if I wasn't there for your big day."

"Sylvie, you didn't know about my condition or about his plan to propose," I whispered, feeling touched. I felt like hugging her. The fact that I couldn't brought tears to my eyes. "Seriously, don't worry about it. It's fine."

"That's right, I didn't know. But I should have shut my stupid mouth, which I never do." She let out a strangled laugh.

I sighed. "That's not you, Sylvie. And honestly, if things were different, I'd rather you told the truth than let me live in denial."

She hesitated. "Even if the truth hurts?"

"Even better," I said, meaning it.

"So, does that mean you'll forgive me?"

"Yes, even though there's nothing to forgive." I nodded,

even though she couldn't see me. "Seriously, no hard feelings. It's water under the bridge."

"Thank God." Her voice sounded so hopeful my chest rose in joy. "Oh wait. Does that mean I'm invited to the wedding?"

"Like I'd ever walk down the aisle without you. Who would be my maid of honor?"

She let out a joyful scream, and it sounded sincere.

"Holy shit. I can't believe you're getting married." Her voice rose into a crescendo of disbelief, and then turned serious again. "No, that was wrong. I did see that coming. I sort of gave up on him after your break-up. You know, I secretly wanted things to work out with you and Jett. You were, and you still are, this perfect couple. And then, bam, you told me you saw him with Tiffany, and I was thinking of my own experiences. I didn't want you to go through hell. I have so many times, and it's not fun."

"I know. I'd have done the same for you." I smiled, touched by her words. "And by that, I mean I'd have tried to verbally slap some sense into you, too."

"We need to celebrate, of course. Like big time," Sylvie said. "Where are you? I'm going to pick you up, and then we'll chat some more. We need to start planning the wedding. It's going to be a full-time job."

I could already feel the bossy vibe wafting from her. Sylvie was going to take control, and there was no stopping her.

"I'm at the gang's headquarters, but you can't visit me now."

"Why not?" Her sudden excitement dropped to disappointment, only to be replaced with a hint of amusement. "Are you and Jett busy?"

With busy, she meant if we were in bed, having sex.

"Yeah, something like that." I smirked as I thought of all the other problems and obstacles that still needed to be dealt with before we could truly enjoy each other.

"Speaking of Jett, what kind of ring did he get you?"

I lifted my hand to admire the sparkling diamond. "You're the expert. You'll have to see for yourself. I'll just say it's beautiful."

I didn't know what made me do it, but I slid the ring off my finger. It was then that I noticed the engraving.

Holy pearls!

"He even engraved it," I muttered in awe. "It says, *With no exceptions, my love for you doesn't need reciprocation to exist.*"

"I so want to get married, too," Sylvie said. "I'm happy for you, Brooke. I really am. This is a dream come true. I know how much you always wanted to get married."

Which was so not the truth.

It had always been Sylvie's secret dream—the one she always adamantly denied.

And it became mine the moment I got pregnant and

realized I wanted a family with Jett.

"Do you remember my vow? The one I took years ago? I promised I'd be your maid of honor, no matter how far we lived from each other."

"Yeah, as a matter of fact I do." I smiled at the memory, unable to stop the moisture in my eyes as I became nostalgic. "You even went as far as denying another bride's request, because you wanted to be mine first."

"Yeah, I did. That is one of my favorite memories," Sylvie whispered, and more silence ensued. Eventually, her voice came low and somewhat weary. "Brooke?"

"Hmm."

"Can you promise that once you get married you won't get all boring and lose touch like so many people do?"

My throat tightened. I could definitely understand her fear.

"I promise we'll be in each other's lives forever," I whispered.

"No matter what?"

"Yeah, no matter what."

"Thank you," she whispered, the relief in her voice carrying down the line. "And now, come on, make me jealous. Describe the ring. And I want every little detail."

"Words don't do it justice. I'm going to send you pictures later."

We talked some more, then I finished the call.

With my back against the bathroom tiles, I turned around and caught a glimpse of Jett standing in the doorway. His shirt was unbuttoned, and he was holding two bags of Chinese food. In the soft light of the bathroom, I saw him for who he was:

My fiancé.

My soon to be husband.

He wasn't just handsome. With his black hair and eyes the color of sin, he was in every way beautiful.

"How did it go?" he asked.

"She's confused, but I think, deep down, she's happy for us."

"I can definitely understand the confusion." He placed a soft kiss on the tip of my nose. "And I'm happy that I got the girl of my dreams, and she so happens to be the mother of my unborn child." He sat the bags down on the counter, and his arms encircled my waist.

I leaned against him, eager and starved for his soothing embrace.

"I love the engraving," I whispered, glancing at my ring again.

"Yeah, I did that for insurance purposes in case you lost it or something. Or if you ever forget my name." He grinned.

"As if you'd ever let me forget you, or your name." I rolled my eyes playfully. "Knowing you, you'll probably have me screaming it at the top of my lungs for the rest of my life, just to be sure."

"So, when are you girls meeting up to plan our wedding?" Jett asked.

"I don't know. Maybe tomorrow."

I stared at him, suddenly feeling anxious. I wanted to see Sylvie, but there were other, more pressing issues on my mind. Interweaving my fingers with his, I looked up. "I want to burn Gina's belongings."

He nodded. "Sure. Let's eat first. I'm going to arrange for us to burn them once it gets dark."

I shook my head. "No, I want to do it now."

"Now?"

I pressed my lips into a tight smile. "The sooner we get rid of them, the sooner I'll feel better."

We weren't just getting rid of stuff that could compromise Jett; I was also getting rid of the feeling that I could lose him.

Moments lost forever.

"Okay, baby. Let's pick up her stuff," Jett said.

Chapter 12

WHEN JETT OPENED the door and we stepped out into the backyard, confusion crossed his face.

"What?" I asked.

"Where's your car?" he asked, scanning the area around us.

"I have no idea." I turned and pointed to the spot where I had parked it. "It was right here."

Jett walked around me and stopped in the empty space where I had pointed, as if my car would miraculously appear between the other parked cars. A giggle escaped my lips. For some reason, the whole situation seemed too funny.

The last thing I needed was for my car to be gone, but I didn't suspect foul play.

"I don't think my car would transform into asphalt." I laughed. "It's not that kind of car."

"You find this funny, Brooke?"

His lips twitched and then spread into a full-blown smile. In the midst of the situation, in the ridiculousness of it all, with him being a possible murder suspect and me a target, hysteria bubbled up. I had no idea what anyone watching might think of us, but I had no doubt we looked like we were high.

"Maybe you forgot it back at my place and took a taxi instead." He titled his head, studying me.

"Yeah, right. As if I'd take a taxi in this neighborhood." A thought struck me when my laughter subsided. "We should ask Brian. Usually, he's guilty as hell." I shrugged because my suggestion made little sense.

"Why would we—" Jett's words were cut off by the sound of a door being thrown open. We turned in time to see Brian stepping out of his car.

"Oh boy," I whispered. "Not again. We should hide in case he decides to interrogate us." I giggled again.

Nothing could pierce my happy bubble.

"Interrogate?" Jett asked. "What are you talking about?"

"He grilled me for at least an hour before letting me see you."

I eyed the big guy nervously. Brian's usual military clothing was gone. Instead, he was wearing a blue mechanic jumpsuit that made him look bigger than he already was. As he stopped in front of us, I noticed how dirty and greasy his hands were. A smile lit up his rugged features. He seemed to be in a good mood, but then Brian was never moody. Crazy, yes, but never moody.

"Hey!" Brian said.

"Hey," Jett answered.

"How's it going?" Brian's gaze swept from me to Jett.

"Where's Brooke's car?" Jett demanded without further ado.

"In the workshop." Just in case we didn't know where it was, Brian pointed his thumb over his shoulder, a lazy grin covering his wide mouth.

"Why would you move it?" Jett's brows shot up as he stepped in front of Brian, which only made Brian laugh.

"Relax, mate. You should have seen the condition it was in. A few more days and it would have taken its last breath on earth. It's a good thing I'm here to take care of an oldie."

Jett looked at him warily, then stormed past him.

"What?" Brian shot me a questioning look, and I shook my head, signaling that I couldn't help him figure Jett out.

We followed Jett through the back door into the generous area Brian called the workshop, which was just another garage adorned with all sorts of mechanical tools and tires and other stuff I couldn't identify even if I wanted.

The moment I stepped through the door, I stopped in mid-stride.

My car was there—or what used to be my car. Someone had taken the liberty of tearing it apart. It was barely more than a skeleton of scrap and metal, just like the other two cars to either side.

My jaw dropped. The wheel was gone. And so were the tires and the seats, but what shocked me the most was the fact that the hood was open and a few things were missing.

"What did you do to my car?" I asked, mortified.

"I gave you a new alternator." Brian smiled proudly. "Your old one was close to dying. Told you already."

Jett ignored him as he rounded the car and opened the trunk. From where I was standing, I saw that the two black bags were gone.

Jett slammed the trunk closed, then turned around to face Brian. "Where are they?" His voice dropped dangerously low, but his face remained expressionless.

"They?" Brian asked, his voice not even hiding the amusement. "What the fuck are you talking about?"

"Don't try to bullshit me." Jett placed himself in front of Brian, his expression hard as stone. "I'll ask you one more time and you better answer. Where. Are. They?"

Grinning, Brian buried his hands in his pockets. "I'm

kidding. I kinda figured she wanted to keep her junk, so I stashed the bags in the blue freezer in the basement."

"In the freezer?" Jett stared at him. "What the fuck!"

Brian shrugged. "I had no idea if she was coming back soon." He glanced at me, the corners of his lips twitching. "Or at all. For all I knew, she might have fled to Mexico, rented a room or something."

"Why would she be heading—" Jett stopped abruptly, eyeing us both. "Am I missing something?"

I gazed from Brian to Jett. "Remember when I told you about him grilling me? Well, I kind of told him."

"Told him what?" Jett asked through gritted teeth.

Brian wrapped one arm around my shoulders. "She told me that she was hiding first-rate evidence in a murder case. How's that for starters?" He turned to me. "Right, Brooke?"

Jett's head snapped in my direction. "You told him that? What the fuck, Brooke!"

"I meant to tell you." I shrugged as I tried to shake Brian's heavy arm off my shoulders.

"Why *didn't* you tell me?" Jett asked, his anger palpable, his stunning green gaze two burning dots.

"Easy, mate." Brian held up a hand. "I asked nicely, and she replied."

A snort escaped my lips. "Yeah, right. You practically forced it out of me. So not nice."

"I think it was a fair deal for entering," Brian said. "There's nothing like a little piece of information to make me happy. I gotta tell you, I didn't expect you'd have the guts to hide it in your car." He seemed genuinely impressed.

I shot him a timid smile. "I had no choice, really."

Ignoring our banter, Jett took my hand possessively and pulled me toward him.

"Did she tell you why?" he asked.

"Because you guys are in trouble?" Brian suggested casually, as if it wasn't a big deal. As if he hadn't expected anything else from us.

Jett opened his mouth to say something, but the ringtone of his phone interrupted him.

"Stay here," Jett said, frowning. "I have to take this."

With that, he left us, slamming the door shut behind him.

Brian and I were alone, his people gone. I peered at him, expecting heavy and uneasy silence.

It never came.

"What?" Brian asked, returning my puzzled look.

I shook my head. "When you asked me why I was here, I didn't think you'd believe me."

"Where I come from, there's a saying. People who stand at your door when it's raining always tell you the truth, so I reckoned you needed help."

I cocked my head. "It wasn't raining."

"No, it wasn't." He smirked. "You got me. Where I come from, there's no such saying. I made it all up. Thought it was clever and all."

I eyed him, curious. "So, how did you figure out it wasn't a lie?"

"Your eyes betrayed you." He winked, and I forced a scowl onto my face. "All right, that was another lie."

"Right." I nodded. This could take a while because Brian didn't seem keen on getting to the point anytime soon.

"You really want to know? Jett's been in a bad mood since your arrival. I reckoned something was wrong and he was in trouble. So when you told me you had first-rate evidence, I thought you knew something he didn't tell me about and took the liberty to open your trunk and put the bags away, just in case, you know, the cops were coming."

"You had no key," I pointed out.

"So?" He shrugged casually. "You think this was the first time I opened a car without one?"

I shook my head, which was rewarded with a chuckle.

"You're fucking unbelievable," I whispered.

"I know."

"I can't believe you took the bags and put them in a frigging freezer," I said, dumbfounded. "Who does that?"

"Trust me. Nobody would look in there." His eyes glimmered with excitement. Knowing Brian, he probably thought his actions were pretty cool.

"It's a good hiding place," I agreed.

His lips twitched before he turned his back to me. "I would have moved everything eventually."

My stomach dropped as I watched him walk over to a shelf and pick up a couple of wrenches and pliers, then return to my car to continue whatever he had been working on.

"Did you look inside?" I asked after a pause.

My question made Brian look up.

"Inside the bags?" Brian shook his head, and his smile disappeared. "No! And I'm not going to ask what's in them."

Narrowing my eyes, I leaned back, unable to hide the doubt in my voice. "So you really didn't look?"

"Nope." He sounded so honest I believed him. If there was ever a doubt, it dissolved quickly the moment I caught his quizzical stare.

"Aren't you curious?" I asked.

"I am. But you'll tell me before it's too late anyway, right?" He gave me a long stare that sent a chill up my spine.

"I want you to know that you're part of our family now, Brooke," he said firmly. "If you're in trouble, you'll get me involved. I know a good place if you need to bury something large."

I stared at him as realization kicked in.

Oh, my God.

"You think I killed someone." I laughed out loud. "I'm crazy, but not so crazy I'd kill someone, Brian." He stared at me, head cocked to the side, as if not sure whether to believe me or not. So I added, "I'm not in that kind of trouble."

"I wasn't talking about you."

My eyes widened as it dawned on me.

"You think Jett killed someone?"

He shrugged. "Well, knowing Jett, it doesn't take long for him to jump the gun. When he's hell-bent on doing something, he really gets it in his head, even if it's a bad idea. It wouldn't really be that much of a surprise."

I frowned.

Heart racing, I turned to him. "What are you talking about?"

For a short moment, silence ensued.

Brian eyed me carefully. I tried to read his expression without much success. And then it dawned on me why he wouldn't just spill the beans, which he usually did.

He had no idea *how much* he could reveal, so he kept quiet.

I rolled my eyes. "Look, Jett told me about my condition, so there's no need for you to protect me from the truth, or whatever." I took a step forward, and my fingers curled around his lower arm. "Please, Brian, if Jett's about to do something stupid, you have to tell me."

His blue eyes pierced mine—the look in them betraying his stony expression.

My heart sputtered in my chest.

"Did Jett say anything about killing someone?" I asked, my tone imploring. As unbelievable as the idea seemed, Jett was unpredictable—and so very protective of me and our unborn child.

"Jett's one of my closest friends, and he really cares about you," Brian said, choosing his words carefully. "He's a good guy, but he's extremely revengeful. So when he says he'll deal with a situation, I usually choose to believe he'll do just that. He's been saying that for weeks, Brooke."

"Nate," I whispered. "You think Jett would kill Nate?"

Brian nodded, and for once, I would have welcomed silence more than the raging thoughts inside my head.

All this time I thought Jett had moved past his anger. All this time I thought Jett had come to peace with the fact that his family wasn't perfect. That his brother was a killer. Worse yet, only a few hours ago, I'd had even jumped to the conclusion that Jett was defending his brother.

That wasn't the case at all. Jett was still fighting his demons.

"What did Jett tell you?" I asked.

"Sorry." Brian smiled apologetically, as though he had

already revealed too much, and moved past me.

So he didn't want to tell me. That, or Jett had asked him not to. Did I even really need it spelled out when I already knew that Jett would hurt anyone who'd dare come after me? Jett was unforgiving and overprotective. He had made that clear on various occasions. I didn't know how far he'd go, but I had no doubt that he was keen to protect what was his at all costs.

Leaning against my car, I watched Brian grab a pair of gloves and a screwdriver, then start busying himself, his face grimacing in concentration. Only then did I notice the dark shadows under his eyes, which in turn made me think of our conversation that morning.

I didn't know what came over me, but I touched his arm again to get his attention. He looked at my fingers as though they were some irritating bugs, his blue eyes probing mine.

"I heard about Tiffany being in the hospital," I started, prying my fingers away from him. "I'm sorry. I hope she'll get well soon."

"She's doing okay, given the circumstances."

Hesitating, I glanced at the door to make sure no one was listening before turning back to him.

"Brian, can I ask you something?"

"That depends." He barely looked up as he unscrewed another thingy for which I had no name with so much fervor I almost feared he might break something.

"It's not about Jett," I added, watching his shoulders relaxing. "Please don't take it the wrong way, but how can you be with someone like her?" I asked in silence. "You know, fearing that she'd cheat. Wondering who she might throw herself at the next time. You seem like a good person, so I don't understand how you can put up with it."

I had been hard on Jett. Most people would have been because it was only human nature in order to emotionally protect oneself. Brian didn't seem to be the most forgiving person in the world. How could he excuse her behavior so easily?

The question had plagued me for some time.

I had to know, if only to understand him. I had to know how someone could love a person who hurt them over and over again.

"I guess for the same reason she returns to me time after time," he said after some pause.

I frowned. "And why is that? Because in her cheating heart, she still loves you after all—and that's all that counts?"

A chuckle escaped his lips. "Honesty and sarcasm. I like that," he said and turned to regard me. "But you couldn't be farther from the truth."

My brows knitted together in confusion. "How so?"

Hesitating, he pulled off his gloves again. He propped a

leg against the wall, then slowly retrieved a pack of chewing gum from his pocket and offered me one. I declined.

"It's a long story," he explained as I watched him open the foil wrapper and shove the chewing gum into his mouth. "To cut it short, the only reason we got back together the first time was that we both hoped at some point we could make it work as a family. It's an Irish thing and has nothing to do with love. I'm the only link to her son, so we try to work it out based on some bullshit belief." He looked up shortly, pride shimmering in his eyes. "He's twelve years old and lives in Ireland with my family."

"Her son?" I asked, suddenly aware of the lump in my throat as I remembered Tiffany's words. "Why would he live with your family? Unless he's your..." My words trailed off as his expression changed to surprise.

"Whoa!" He held out his hand, and the skin around his eyes crinkled in amusement. "Did you think it was Jett's kid?"

Heat scorched my cheeks, the spreading blush across my chin giving me away. It was too late to lie.

He had caught me, and I only had two options. Admit that I had been jealous or deny everything, which would make me look weak.

"He isn't?"

"No, Brooke," he said with a curious glance at me. "Tiffany wanted to give our son up for adoption when she was sixteen, because we had no money, no support, not even a safe place to stay. My family took him in, and now they're raising him as their own. That was the hardest decision I ever made."

I stared at him, lost for words.

All this time, I had assumed that Tiffany went through with an abortion or had a miscarriage. It never crossed my mind that she and Brian went back longer than she and Jett, that she had to give her child away; and how difficult it must have been for her as a mother. Not having the means to care for her child and being forced to give him away was horrible.

I couldn't imagine living without my child, and she wasn't born yet.

In the gloomy silence, his eyes probed mine as he paused for a second, probably considering his words. Eventually, something changed in his gaze, and I knew he was about to share his story with me—a story so private I could feel my heart shattering with each word he spoke.

"She hasn't seen him since the day he was born. He has no idea that I'm his father," Brian said.

For the first time, I thought I caught something in his voice.

Pain.

Suffering.

Longing.

"Giving up her child destroyed our relationship. I don't think she'll ever get over the guilt of not having seen him grow up." He shook his head slowly, his hazy gaze reminiscent of the past. "Nowadays, when I look at her, I know she wants to see him, but she can't bring herself to do it, because she's a mess. She doesn't want him to see her like this."

"She could get help," I said.

Maybe I could help.

I wanted to utter the words, but I bit my lip instead, holding them back because it made no sense to tell Brian. I needed to tell her. Maybe she needed a friend who understood the way she felt as a mother.

"She's tried so many times, you have no idea. You need to forgive her," he said, his eyes not leaving mine. "I know she has no excuse for trying to get it on with Jett, but she's an alcoholic and hasn't been herself for a long time. Giving up her son changed her. It changed our relationship, and it changed her love for me. Even though it was her who came up with the idea of giving our son away, I was the one who pushed her to go through with it. She never forgave me." He sighed, and for a moment, I thought I glimpsed moisture in his eyes. "Anyway, like I said, it's a long story."

"Brian, I had no idea. About your son. About Tiffany. Jett didn't say anything," I whispered.

"I should hope so. It's most certainly not his place." He

shrugged again. "Not many people know about this part of my past, and Jett didn't tell you because I asked him not to a long time ago. Anyway, there's not much point in bringing something up that you can't change, right?" He glanced back at me and smiled gently. "It's not a story I'm proud of. I don't know what's in those bags and what you're hiding for him, but I can see why he loves you, even if he hadn't told me the night before."

He loves me.

Jett had confessed his love to me in spite of our fight and disagreements. In spite of the fact that he didn't even know whether our relationship would make it.

My heart fluttered.

All those emotions I had for him came back like a big wall crushing me. It took me every ounce of willpower not to say that I loved Jett, too. My heart gave little jumps as I thought of him. After all the jealousy that I thought would consume me at the mere mentioning of Tiffany's name, I found myself smiling with joy.

Joy—that Tiffany wasn't the bad person I imagined her to be.

Joy—that there most certainly was a reason why she kissed Jett.

And, most importantly, joy that Jett never stopped loving me during our ugly fight. It was proof to me that Jett would stand by me no matter what.

"And congratulations." He smiled and motioned at my ring. "We're having a secret engagement party tomorrow, which I'm not supposed to tell you about, but you have this uncanny ability to pull secrets out of people."

I laughed and glanced at my beautiful ring. "Thank you for telling me," I whispered, not referring to the party.

When I looked up, Brian had already turned away, his footsteps thudding as he crossed the garage. For some reason, I felt as though I had glimpsed a new side of him. A side that didn't scare me.

Maybe someday Brian and I would become friends. Or maybe we already were.

Chapter 13

THE FLAMES SENT sparks high up into the sky. We stood there, watching the fire in the back yard of the gang's quarters. Jett's arms were around me, pulling me close, cuddling me against his hard chest, his lips nestled at the back of my neck. Brian and four of his people were standing behind us. None of them asked any questions before they threw the black bags into the bonfire, the wild flames savaging the contents.

The fire flared and died.

Eventually, people began to leave, until Jett and I were alone.

As I watched the dark ashes, tears rose to my eyes.

Those had been Gina's things—a woman I had known for only two days, but for some reason I had liked her.

She didn't deserve what happened to her.

Of course, there was still a distinct possibility that I had been wrong, and the bags belonged to someone else, but that didn't matter much.

Life ended in the blink of an eye.

I knew next to nothing about Gina, but she had left sadness behind.

She had left emptiness in the hearts of those who loved her.

"You okay?" Jett whispered behind me.

"I am. Just a little sad about her, that's all," I whispered back, my glance fixed on the dying fire. "Did you hear from Sam?"

"Not yet." He paused a little, and I sensed a change in topic. "My assistant called to confirm our attendance at the charity fashion show."

I turned around, and my eyes found him. "When will it start?"

Jett glanced at his cell phone, then back at me. "We should head back inside now. Particularly if you want to take the time to check out my former room before we leave."

"I know where your room..." My words trailed off as I got the hint. "Oh. But we've already done it twice today."

213

"No, not with you as my fiancée." He tilted his head, and something tugged between my legs. Though his face was bathed in semi-darkness, I could feel his desire as strongly as before. "What do you think?"

"Will you ever get rid of your sex addiction?" I teased, surprised at how something as simple as an unspoken invitation to have him inside me could make my skin prickle and my heartbeat speed up.

"Can't say that I harbor any plans, but you never know." He leaned forward until his lips brushed my earlobe. "I've been told all good things are three," he whispered. "I have a very good idea of what I want to do with you. It doesn't even have to involve the sexy lingerie I got you."

***

I've always known that life can both suck and surprise in the same instant. I just had no idea how much it could. When you're lying in the arms of your lover, praying that the moment will never pass, you should never trust that everything will stay the same.

One wrong step.

That's all that ever matters.

One look back, and I should have known it was my time to run.

But I had been too stupid to think beyond that special

moment.

Or maybe I didn't mind what lay beyond.

I was newly engaged with grand plans of a wedding and renewed hopes for the future. My heart had been revived, and my faith strengthened by recent events.

I was in love.

I was in lust.

And I was absolutely in no mood to talk to strangers, which is what I was sure I'd be forced to do at the charity event.

"God, the next few hours will be hard." I let out a sigh, pushing up from my lying position. "How am I supposed to make it without this?" I pointed at Jett's naked body, my eyes drinking him in, my mind marveling at how perfect he was.

"Yeah?" Jett's brows shot up, amused. "And you call me a sex addict."

I slapped his shoulder and let my fingers glide over his skin. "To Jupiter. That's how far your confidence will grow if you don't learn to rein it in."

"That's a good name," he said, suddenly absentminded.

"Good name for what?"

Jett leaned back, resting against the pillows, his arms crossed behind his head, a thoughtful expression on his face.

"If we have another girl, it'll be the perfect name for

her."

"What? No way." I laughed out loud, then stopped when I saw his face. "Wait, you're serious?" He nodded. "No way in hell, Jett. We'll never name any child Jupiter. Besides, who says I want another one? I'm still carrying this one, huffing and puffing as we're speaking, and you're already thinking ahead."

His laugh was interrupted by the ringtone of his phone.

"Excuse me." I watched him as he straightened and grabbed his phone from the nightstand. His gaze briefly brushed me before locking on the caller ID.

Turning his back on me, he picked up.

There was only one call Jett would always accept.

"Sam." For three minutes, Jett said nothing else, just listened, his shoulders slightly tense.

I held my breath as I tried to tune in, without much success.

Eventually, Jett's voice cut through the silence.

"How?" He shook his head angrily. "How is that possible?" Whatever Sam had said, it must have made Jett pissed off because waves of anger were wafting from him. "No, I'll deal with it. Just send it over as soon as you can...No, there's no need. I'll take care of it."

With that, he snapped the phone shut, his back still turned to me as silence returned to the room. I watched him, seconds ticking by.

"So, what did Sam say?" I asked when it became obvious that Jett harbored no intention of sharing the news with me.

My heart thudded in my chest at the possibilities of what Sam could have said.

Had the tests shown that Gina had been drugged?

Of course, she had been drugged. If not, it meant I had been the only one targeted, which, in turn, would mean Gina had been involved.

"The same drug was found in Gina's body," Jett murmured and turned around. His beautiful face twisted into something I thought I'd never see.

Pain.

Anger.

Worry.

All at once.

He grew silent—the kind of silence that sent a chill up my spine.

"What?" I asked, somehow unable to grasp the meaning of his words.

Jett looked at me for one long, hard moment, and in that second I realized there was more.

I stared at him, the cold sensation inside my stomach turning to boiling heat only to change to ice again.

What could be so terrible that Jett was afraid to tell me?

I waited patiently.

When he began to speak again, the words were as chilling as death entering the room.

"Nate's gone." Jett's voice lowered to a whisper. "Sam called to say that a police offer was shot during his escape."

Chapter 14

A SCREAM BUILT in my throat, but the sound remained trapped inside my mouth. To claim that I was shocked by something as simple as a few words was an understatement. I feared for my life, for my baby, for Jett, and that fear enclosed my mind and body, rendering me unable to form a coherent thought.

Waking up that morning, I thought I had experienced the worst. Then, after Jett's proposal, my life and relationship would finally move on to a better place, that maybe we could leave the past behind once and for all and start preparing ourselves for something wonderful.

A life together.

A family.

But now, based on the recent events, all the facts led to one assumption.

One scary conclusion:

It wasn't over.

It never had been—the past few hours of joy easily shattered by something as simple as words.

I thought with Nate being in prison and most of the club members exposed and arrested, the police had put a stop to the club's activities. But that didn't seem to be the case. Gina was dead; maybe even others. The nightmare seemed to continue. It always would.

Nate's release might be the beginning of another nightmare, where the worst was still to come. I had no idea how to stop him, how to prepare myself for what I feared the most. In particular, the high-ranked club members had connections, people who knew how to appear in silence, doing their dirty jobs, and then disappear just as quickly and invisibly—like ghosts. Protecting myself and the people I loved sounded insane—a plan doomed for failure.

"Good Lord." I stared at Jett, noticing the throbbing nerve visible beneath the soft skin around his eyes. He looked tired. At some point, dark circles had framed his beautiful green gaze. "How is that possible? I thought he was under surveillance."

My body trembled; resignation was palpable in my voice.

I hated weakness; I hated not having the strength to pretend. All of my energy was gone, dissipated, as if saying Nate's name had the power to suck it out of my body.

"I don't know," Jett said quietly. "All Sam said was that he found a hole in their system and took advantage of it."

"Good Lord," I repeated and crossed my arms over my chest. The shivers running through me came hard, wave after wave, destroying any hope that we'd ever find peace. My muscles were tense, aching from the effort, as a cold sensation washed over me like an icy waterfall.

"The police officer..." I couldn't even say the words.

"Sam said he might survive."

Might.

I swallowed the lump lodged in my throat.

What if he wouldn't? He could have been someone's father, husband, brother, and lover. Someone who worked hard to protect *innocents*. Someone who loved and had been loved.

"Brooke." Jett cleared his throat. His hands cupped my face, his gaze searching mine.

My tears began to pool at the corners of my eyes.

Stupid tears that just wouldn't stop.

I closed my eyes in the hope Jett wouldn't catch them.

"This doesn't change anything," he whispered firmly. "I won't let him hurt you. Nor will my friends. You know they stand behind us in every way."

"I know," I whispered. "But I'd rather have him locked up than roaming free and hurting more people."

Jett's arms engulfed me. But even in his soothing presence, my body continued to shiver.

"He'll make a mistake, and they will catch him again."

"How can you be so sure about that?" I looked up, more in search of his support than to express my anger. "He has so many connections."

His shoulders slumped a little bit. Before he even said the words, I knew he was being optimistic. "Well, that's the thing," Jett said. "I hope I'm right. Knowing Nate and his tendency to avoid getting his hands dirty, he probably asked for help. The more people get involved, the greater the risk that someone will make a mistake. Sooner or later, the police will track him down. Just wait and see. The whole thing will be over before it even began."

They were supposed to be words emitting strength and faith.

For a moment, I wanted to believe them.

If only my brain would stop telling me that it was a mediocre attempt. Jett didn't have any superpowers. Like Gina, Jett was human.

Sexy and perfect—but still not invincible.

And he couldn't predict the future.

Like the police officer, he could be shot. If they never found Nate, I'd never be safe from him. And neither would

Jett. Knowing Nate and his wicked obsession with power and death, he might lay low for a while. But eventually, he'd come after Jett and me. It'd only be a matter of time until he reached his friends and found new ones who shared his sick fantasies.

I nodded, but the motion lacked conviction. Jett must have sensed my fears because he continued with more vengeance than I wanted him to have, "If he so much as steps in your way, I'll shoot him. I'll get Kenny to track him down."

I frowned. "I'm not sure I want you to get involved."

"It's too late for that. I'm already too deep into this." His glance locked on me. "If someone tries to scare you, that's my God damn business. I swear the moment I see him, I'm going to kill him."

My stomach twisted.

"He's your brother," I reminded him.

"No, he's not." He exhaled a sharp breath. "He lost that privilege a long time ago."

Taking in his words, I shook my head slowly. "You're not your brother, Jett. You're not like Nate. Compared to him, you're a good man."

"No." He shook his head, his mouth pressing into a tighter line. "That's where you're wrong. I'm only good when I'm with you." He looked up, his eyes meeting mine. "Nate and I aren't so different. The moment he messes with my personal life and threatens you, I can't just stand there and do nothing. I can't just wait for the cops to do their job, and I sure as fuck can't wait for something to happen. I won't let it be too late." He placed one finger under my chin and forced me to meet his eyes. His stare was determined, his tone chilling. "You have absolutely no idea what I'd do to him. Someone needs to stop him. And that someone is me."

My pulse began to pound against my temples.

No, I had absolutely no idea what Jett would do to him.

But judging from my earlier conversation with Brian, I had a good idea where it would land Nate. The possibility of Jett getting hurt or killed along the way was there.

"Jett, no!" I said. "Promise you won't do anything stupid."

"I can't do that," he said firmly. "I'd be lying if I told you I wanted to see him alive. He…" His words broke as anger consumed him. "He betrayed me; he betrayed my father. He went too far. It's all my fault."

I stared at him in shock. "It's not your fault, Jett."

"It is," Jett retorted firmly. "I'm the one who grew up with him. I should have known him better, but…I underestimated him and that was a mistake."

A muscle worked his jaw, but he said no more. And I knew then that even though he was wrong, there was nothing I could do to help ward off the demons consuming his soul. The very demons that had made him lose all faith in people. The demons that didn't allow him to feel peace and trust and safety.

I wrapped my arms around him and placed my head against his chest, hoping that my presence would give him as much comfort as he did to me.

"You couldn't have stopped him even if you'd wanted to, Jett," I murmured under my breath.

"See, that's where you're wrong," Jett said. "I could have done something before someone got killed. God knows it takes planning to execute what he's done. And if what you say is true, and these were Gina's things, then I believe he'd planned to frame me for a long time. He wanted to get rid of me, and now I might be paying the price." He brushed a hand over his face, his voice oozing danger and frustration. "That son of a bitch wants me to miss the birth of our daughter and our wedding. He knows how much you mean to me, and he thinks he can get away with anything. But he forgets that I could have killed him right there and then, when you were alone with him, and I didn't. That's nobody's fault but my own. If I could turn back time, I know what I'd do."

I placed a hand on his shoulder and trailed my fingers down his arm, marveling at how smooth and taut his skin felt.

"Jett?" I said, infusing as much confidence as I could

into my tone. "Someday he'll get what he deserves. But it won't be you who serves justice. Do you understand?" He remained silent, so I continued, "I don't want you to get involved, Jett, because that's exactly what he wants. Don't give him the satisfaction. It's not worth the trouble. Like you said, the cops will find him in no time. He'll get caught. It'll probably be over before it's even begun." I repeated his words, this time almost believing them.

Jett looked at me long and hard, his green eyes darkening. The aura he radiated was so strong I would have given anything to know his thoughts. Even though chaos was still surrounding us, his anger began to ebb, and eventually, peace settled in his gaze.

His face softened, and at last, his shoulders relaxed.

"You're right," he whispered. "He wants me to come after him. He might think he's clever, but he should never have shot that cop. Now they'll be after him. If they get him, they'll probably put a bullet straight into his head and call it self-defense."

"Yes," I agreed. "You're probably right."

He lifted my fingers to his mouth. Goose bumps covered my skin as his lips brushed over me, kissing my knuckles then the inside of my palm. I felt relief that Jett and I were seeing eye-to-eye, but more than that, I was hopeful that, whatever differences in viewpoints we might encounter in the future, we could work through them.

"I'd never ever let anything come between us, Brooke," he whispered in his sexy Southern voice. "If I can't get him away from you, then I'll find a way to get you away from him or else I'm forced to get rid of him. We'll be taking a little vacation."

His suggestion took me by surprise. For a few seconds, I thought it was over.

Going away...that was exactly what I wanted. But was it really that simple? Could we leave it all behind?

"You want to go away?" I asked, unsure what to make of it.

"Yes." He nodded his head. "I've already booked a flight to Las Vegas. We'll leave in two days."

My lips curled into a smile.

I couldn't help it.

"Why there?"

"No idea." His smile matched mine. "Maybe because Las Vegas is sin city, and my obsession with you is kind of sinful. Besides, you said you've never been, and I thought it was about time you traveled a bit before our kid starts to demand all your attention."

I swallowed hard. "Yes, makes sense."

"After Vegas, we'll head back to Italy," he added casually, his glance never leaving mine.

My smile vanished. I eyed him carefully.

"I'm not sure that's a good idea, Jett. It'd look like

you're on the run," I said.

"I'm not, because as far as things stand, I don't know anything about anyone." He smiled knowingly. "Baby, I'm not letting you stay here. It isn't even a question; it's a demand. NY is not good for you—at least not as long as Nate's investigation's pending. We both need to head back to Bellagio, back to where things were simple." He sat down, then took my hands, pulling me onto his lap. I wrapped my arms around his neck and settled as comfortably as my growing belly would allow.

"It's a good time to take a vacation," Jett continued. "A break from everything to focus on our engagement." His hand rubbed my back, the motion comforting and soothing, easing some of the pressure that had built inside me. "I only want what is best for you, and right now, I want you to feel safe. I tried to protect you from the ugliness that's been all around us, but my attempts got me nowhere. I don't see a reason why we should be hiding."

"It's okay," I whispered. "I'm used to ugliness. Particularly since it keeps popping up in my life, no matter what."

I couldn't pull the bitter tone out of my voice.

It was the truth. The ugly, bitter truth.

I bit my lip in a desperate attempt to stop the tears from welling up.

"That doesn't make it okay," he said an instant before

his lips brushed my naked shoulders. His kiss relaxed me, if only for the time being. "Trust me. Taking an oversea's trip is a good idea. Today, let's forget all our problems. Let's forget about Gina and focus only on us. It is as good a time as any to attend the NYC charity fashion show."

My breath hitched.

Oh. My. God.

"Did you say the NYC charity fashion show?" I choked on my words. "But…I thought this was nothing special."

"It must have slipped my mind." Jett grinned.

"Oh my god."

The NYC charity fashion show was swarming with journalists and celebrities. It was one of the most established and celebrated events of the year. I knew because Sylvie read about it in her magazines and then left those magazines lying around for me to dispose of.

Jett wasn't just a billionaire; he was one of the youngest and most successful businessmen in the world. So it was only natural that he'd be invited and the media would want to take pictures.

"Is this really a good idea?" I asked. "What if the cops are looking for you? The place is probably crawling with security and bodyguards and people who know you."

"If anyone dares to say one wrong word, I'll call my lawyers." His tone was nonchalant, as though gossip didn't bother him, as if he was used to false accusations and people talking. "If anyone asks, we both ditched the club on Sunday to spend the night together at your place."

Which was kind of true, but—

"You know we can't prove that," I said flatly.

"No, you can't, but I can." His lips cracked into a smile. I looked up at him, confused.

"What do you mean?"

He started pressing buttons on his phone, then let out something that resembled, "Yeah, that's it."

I craned my neck to get a better look, but there was no need for it because Jett turned the screen for me to see.

I stared at it, unable to comprehend the meaning of the picture.

"I took it the night Gina died," he explained. "There's a timestamp and everything. This should answer any questions."

With trembling fingers, I took the phone from his hand, my eyes fixed on the picture of me, sleeping half-naked.

My hair was spread around me like a halo, and my abdomen was exposed. Even though the image was small, I could see that wasn't anyone's belly.

It was the body of a woman who looked very pregnant.

For a few seconds, I was lost for words.

"Why didn't you tell me?" I asked, unable to place my emotions. First, there was confusion, then relief, and now I couldn't wait to seek answers to the array of questions inside my head.

"No idea." He grinned. "Maybe because we fought and you would've asked me to delete them."

"I most certainly would have done that." I stared at the picture again, shaking my head. "I probably would've had a point. Look at this, I'm huge. And..." I frowned as I stared at what might be a stretch mark, but you couldn't see those so clearly in a picture, could you?

I had no time to find out because Jett pulled the phone away.

"You're beautiful," he said with that sparkle in his eyes that made me adore him even more.

Tears began to trickle down my cheeks. But this time, they were not caused by fear. I was genuinely touched—not by Jett's words, but his actions.

Jett inched closer and brushed his fingers over my cheeks, the motion gentle and soothing.

"Now you know why I never believed there'd be a trial," he whispered. "Like I said, whoever's trying to frame me has no proof that would ever stand in court. I'm not saying this picture would solve everything, because let's face it, people love headlines. They love scandals. They love making money by dragging other people's names through the dirt. But this"—he held up his phone—"is all the proof I need that I wasn't anywhere near her. You have nothing to worry about, Brooke."

"I'm so happy," I said, relieved. "I can't even believe I'm saying this after finding out that Nate's gone, but it's true. How come you didn't tell me this before?"

He shrugged nonchalantly. "That night, I didn't know about Gina. When you told me, I explained that I didn't kill her."

"But you could have shown me, and I would have believed you." I eyed him carefully, eager to catch his expression. "Don't tell me it slipped your mind, because I know that's not the case. Nothing ever slips your mind."

"Brooke." He paused and sighed. I looked up from the picture to take in his thoughtful expression. "Would it really have made a difference?"

My heart gave an enormous thud. The silence in the room became ominous.

"What do you mean?" I asked.

"Our relationship needs to be built on trust." His voice sounded serious, almost reproachful. For some reason, I felt scolded. "All I'm saying is that I don't feel like I have to prove anything to anyone. Either you believe me or you do not. I wanted to see if you could."

"Right." I exhaled slowly as I tried to process his words. "So, it was all a test?"

"No." He shook his head. "I'd never go as far as testing you. I'd rather call it a leap of faith in our relationship. In our love. That one last step before marriage."

"I don't understand." I shook my head, suddenly feeling hurt. "Why wouldn't I believe you?"

"I needed to see if you'd stand by me," he said, and I stiffened. "Most people would falter and run when they think their partner might have committed murder. Not you, Brooke. I *knew* you would stand by me. I wanted to see how it'd turn out."

"To see if I'd crack."

"Yes," he said quietly. "I never gave a fuck about the trial. Without any physical proof, they never had a case in the first place. But the last step in everyone's relationship before marriage is proving that real trust exists. That it's there for the future. All I wanted was to make sure that you trusted me and loved me for who I am."

"I don't know what to say."

"Nothing. There is no need to say anything because in simplicity lies wholeness." He grinned. "Anyway, I took a snapshot every week when you were asleep. And may I say you sleep soundly."

Soundly?

I opened my mouth to comment when he started flipping picture over picture.

Holy cow.

Most of them had indeed been taken while I was asleep or in the shower.

My jaw dropped.

"I'm at a loss for words," I said, stunned. "I had no idea you could be this sneaky."

He laughed out loud, and something flickered in his gaze.

Was that pride?

Holy shit.

He was proud of himself!

"Really, you left me with no choice, Brooke. Remember the night you told me you hated the idea of becoming big. Well, it was the night I decided I looked forward to seeing your body grow, change, and so the decision to document that change was born. I wanted something like a digital scrapbook. A keepsake." He pointed at his phone. "All those pictures are here to help us remember our first pregnancy. Once the journey's over and Treasure's born, I'll print them all. I can't wait to out us as a couple tonight and introduce the whole world to my new fiancée."

My breath hitched in my throat as I watched him walk to the door. "You want to—"

He stopped at the door and turned around. "Yes, make it all public, official, in case you didn't get the hint."

"But…" I paused, lost for words. "The charity fashion show is huge. There are journalists and cameras. The whole world will know."

He nodded slowly. "That's right."

"And we would be in the papers." I gulped hard as I

realized I had no idea what to wear.

"Exactly, which is why…" He glanced at his watch, his expression turning all business like again. "You better hurry. You only have fifteen minutes until the driver picks us up."

"Fifteen minutes? Are you kidding me?" I groaned. As usual, Jett was completely clueless. No woman could get ready in fifteen minutes. It was literally impossible. Besides, he forgot one tiny fact. "I have nothing to wear."

"So you think." He grinned. "If I were you, I'd look in the closet, where there's a box waiting for you." He nodded his head toward the closet. And then he headed out, leaving me with a whole set of thoughts and questions I had no time to consider because I had to get ready.

Damn.

I had no idea where to start.

Chapter 15

NEVER TELL A woman she only has fifteen minutes to get ready because there's no way she can do it. Not even when a sexy rock star is standing in front of the door. And the knowledge that she's about to attend one of the biggest fashion events in New York City won't exactly help.

First, there was the hair. A whole lot of hair that I couldn't ever get straight and glossy—not without spending at least two hours staring at my reflection while fighting with strand after strand and lots of straightening serum.

Second, oh my God.

I held up the piece of fabric.

Did Jett *have* to go for what could only be described as

the most extravagant cocktail dress? The dress, a mixture of green with shimmery blue, was stunning, no doubt about that. Black lace was draped over the silky material, sheathing my body.

But, fuck, it was so tight that I feared the delicate fabric would rip if I so much as took a few steps, let alone ascended a flight of stairs or, God forbid, bent forward. It didn't help at all that the split on the left side rode up my thigh, or that the sparkling accents around my waist made me feel like a peacock among swans.

Too daring.

Too bold.

With a sigh, I slipped my feet into my high heels—a shimmering dark green to match the dress—and turned around to regard myself in the mirror.

Another knock rapped at the door.

"Brooke." Jett's voice echoed through the bathroom, disrupting my thoughts. "We need to get going, babe."

"Just a minute."

"You already said that five minutes ago," he said, his tone carrying a hint of amusement.

"Just another minute, Jett." Frustrated, I ran my hand through my hair, but the curls bounced back with more fervor. I let my hand sink in desperation and stood back to inspect myself in the mirror, shaking my head.

Whatever I did, I'd never look perfect—for the cameras.

The prospect of being photographed with Jett made me nervous, more so now that I was his fiancée.

I uncapped my lipstick and blotted more color onto my lips.

Jett knocked again, and before I could stop him, the door was thrown open.

"I'm not going to wait any—" He broke off mid-sentence. I turned around, more out of exasperation than irritation.

"I said one minute, Jett. I'm really not finished." My gaze caught his stare, and my body heated up instantly. "What?" My fingers raked through my hair. His stare—hungry and intense—made me feel self-conscious.

"Wow." He let out a surprised breath. "You look beautiful."

I smiled shyly. "Thank you."

He took a lazy step forward and curled a strand of my hair around his finger. I felt the need to wrap it all in a low side bun, but his proximity stopped me.

Even though we had been dating for a while, I still had trouble breathing whenever he was around. There was something about him—about his dominating height, his stance, his scent—that made me want to run away and undress him, all at the same time.

His finger lifted my chin to meet his gaze.

"I need to ask you something. How did you know it

wasn't me?" He paused, his expression darkening. "Every other person would have doubted me. It's something I have been wondering about lately."

His question took me by surprise. I leaned back, taken aback.

How could I possibly explain to him what felt right to me?

"Call it a gut feeling."

"How so?

I brushed my hair behind my ears, considering my words. "After I found out you had paid off my debts, I drove to your apartment. It was a complete mess. At first, I assumed the police had been there, but then I discovered another woman's clothes and I assumed you spent time with her—" I trailed off as I glanced at him.

"You assumed I had someone over."

The telltale heat of a blush covered my face. There was no point in denying that part. "At first. Yes."

"Why did you take her things?" Another question caught me off guard.

"I don't know." My voice broke. Why had I indeed? "Once I realized they were Gina's, I didn't want you to get into trouble, I guess. If the cops found the stuff at your place, it would have been impounded as evidence."

Jett shook his head in amazement. "I can't believe you took such a risk, Brooke. What were you going to do with it?"

"Honestly, I have no idea." I shrugged because, really, I had no idea. It hadn't been the best of plans. "I guess you rub off on me."

"Would you still have done it if you had known I was going to Chicago?" Jett asked quietly.

I raised my brows. "Of all the questions you could ask me, this is the one that bothers you the most?"

"I'm just surprised, that's all. Would you have done it?"

"Yes. I guess." I bit my lip, thinking. "It felt right."

"Why?" He looked at me intently. "Assuming I was cheating on you, did you really think I deserved to be saved?"

"But that's the thing, you weren't cheating."

"True, but what if that had been the case?"

I frowned. "Would I? Did I? Had I? What's the point of all the questioning? You didn't." I laughed nervously, afraid that my earlier fears would creep back up on me.

They didn't.

"Okay," he continued, stubborn as a mule as usual. "Let's assume I had been. Would you still have done it?"

I cleared my throat to get rid of the lump. Finally, I let out an exasperated sigh and dropped my arms in mock annoyance. "Yes, I believe so."

"But why, Brooke? Help me understand."

"Maybe, because deep down, I knew you were a good

man, Jett. Or maybe I wanted you to be good. In the end, that's all that matters. But my strong trust in you isn't why I handled the situation the way I did. I did it because I love you. I wanted you to be safe, regardless of whether we were together or not. Call it unconditional love."

He smiled, and then he cupped my face in his big hands, holding me the way only he could. "I'm glad we're on the same page, Brooke, because I would have done the same thing for you, even if you broke my heart." He paused. When he spoke again, his voice was gentle, infused with something I couldn't pinpoint. "We have this intensive chemistry. Don't you think we can call it destiny?"

I stared at him. "You believe in destiny?"

"No." He shook his head. "I believe meeting you was fate. I believe that relationships don't stop working. I believe people just give up. I believe that we still have a lot going for us. While we'll always have our differences, I'll never give up on this relationship, and neither are you, Brooke, because after everything we've been through, I believe you're the one woman for me. "

"Does that mean you'll stay in New York?"

He returned my smile. "Did you really think you could get rid of me that easily?"

"I don't know. Can I?"

His lips twitched.

"You can try and see how it works out."

"Okay." Without a pause, I turned on my heels and ran.

But he was faster.

He caught up in no time and wrapped his arms around me, spinning me around.

I squealed.

Planting a kiss on my cheek, he whispered, "No chance. Next time you try to outwit me, make sure to run faster."

"Not when I look like a whale. Maybe I'll try again when I'm in a car."

"I'd find you wherever you are," Jett said. "I'm like one of the best racers in the world. Not to mention very good at finding people."

Yeah, he had made that part pretty obvious on various occasions.

I shook my head. "You know, following someone is kind of creepy."

"I'm fully aware of that." His mouth curved into a wicked smile. "But in my defense, I'll say that I'm only doing it because I'm insanely infatuated with you. You don't know the lengths to which I would go to have you by my side."

"Really?"

"Yeah, really." He placed a soft kiss on my skin.

"How far?" I asked, a bit out of breath.

"What?"

"How far would you go?" I challenged him.

He put me down, but his hands stayed on my hips.

"I'd die for you, Brooke. That's how much I love you. I'd kill for you, and I'd make sure you have everything that makes you happy, even if that means staying away from you, watching you move on, living your life without me. All beginnings are hard, but you know what, endings are harder. Knowing it's over and being apart from you would be a sure way to make me kill myself. But I would have done it if you wanted me out of our life."

My heart beat faster. "Don't say that."

"But it's true." His finger brushed my lips. "I want to be honest, Brooke. Before I met you, I didn't believe in love and in the whole love and romance declaration thing. Heck, I used to make fun of the whole Romeo and Juliet stuff, because for me love was a myth." He laughed, as though the idea was still alien to him. "I always thought people deluded themselves. The more they loved me, the more I felt caged in and wanted to run away from them." He shrugged. "What's worse, for a long time women were coming and going. They were only there to get my wants fulfilled. They obeyed me, followed me. Did everything I wanted, but I still wasn't happy, nor did I care enough about them to keep them close."

He brushed my hair out of my face, regarding me intently. When I didn't reply, he continued.

"I know it sounds bad. I admit I was an asshole for

using them without having the intention of keeping them."
His eyes locked with mine, searching for something I
couldn't give. Maybe forgiveness. Maybe understanding.
"But I'm not the same man anymore, Brooke. The player in
me is gone. For what it's worth, meeting you changed me.
You made me a better a man. I would never leave you. No
matter how bad things might be between us, I'll always be
there for you." He frowned when he saw my expression.
"You don't believe me?"

"A few days ago when I called, I thought you didn't care
about me," I admitted. "I was sure you had moved on."

"You think I could ever move on so easily?" he asked,
surprised.

"I'm not gonna lie. I think you can. You're a man with
needs," I replied. "Needs that don't care whether your
girlfriend's pregnant. Needs that could turn ugly if you
don't get what you want."

"Brooke, my needs don't define me." He stared at me,
his expression softened. "Needs don't make me. It's want.
And what I want is you. I never had such a feeling before."

"And once I grow old and ugly? Once this pregnancy
changes my body? Or once things get boring, because you
know they will. It happens in every relationship," I asked,
both hoping for and fearing the truth.

"Especially then. I very much look forward to those
times, because I know we'll be going through them

together." His hand rested on my arm. The gentle touch of his fingertips tracing contours on my skin sent shivers through me. "Every scar tells a story. Every change is proof of something that you've overcome. It's evidence of our past together." He cupped my face, his eyes locking on me. "You're perfect, Brooke. You will never be ugly because I fell in love with your soul."

"What about problems? Because you know they'll surface eventually."

He shook his head. "Problems don't matter. What matters to me is that you're by my side, experiencing them with me, while we stay together."

I smiled. I wanted to believe him, and for once, I was ready to do just that. "I think I'd like that."

" | And I want you to live with me, Brooke. I know you already moved some stuff over to my place, but I mean, move in with me permanently so we can raise our child together. Is that something you'd want, too, now that we're engaged?"

I stared at him, my heart skipping several beats.

Was this seriously happening?

We had spent weeks choosing a name, schools, education, but we had never discussed what would happen to *us* after our child's birth. That had worried me because I had no idea which direction our relationship would be taking. A slow smile spread across my face as the knots in my stomach began to dissipate, replaced by a feeling of happiness.

"I would love to," I whispered. "But your apartment—"

"Is not ideal for a child, I know," he cut me off. "Give me a few days and I'll think of something." He smiled gently, picking a strand of my hair and twisting it between his fingers. "It's no longer just about us, Brooke. It's all about you, and me, and our baby. We'll soon be a family."

That sounded like heaven.

I smiled and brushed my fingertips over his face, tracing the contours of his chin.

"You're really beautiful, Brooke. I mean it," he whispered, leaning into me. His warm breath caressed my earlobe, and for a moment, I closed my eyes to savor the sensation. When his arm slid around my waist, I almost feared the charity event would take place without us. "You look exactly like the kind of woman I want to marry."

"You don't look so bad, either," I whispered, rising on my toes to nibble on his neck.

Now that was a big, fat lie.

Jett looked absolutely breathtaking. Stunningly gorgeous.

The dark suit he was wearing brought out the mysterious glint in his eyes. Even though I was used to seeing him dressed for the occasion by now, something about him was different tonight.

He seemed so—

Dark.

Confident.

Broody, even.

He was probably in one of those moods that turned his eyes a darker shade of green and gave him a haunted look.

The kind of mood that always made my panties wet.

Clasping my hands behind his neck, I placed a soft kiss on his lips. His answer was instant.

Burning ardor.

His mouth briefly met mine, then moved on to my neck, his tongue trailing down to my exposed shoulder.

"I thought we needed to go," I whispered and instantly cursed myself for not being able to keep my mouth shut.

"Damn." He pulled away with a pained expression on his handsome face. "If we weren't already late, I would fuck you right here and now."

"Now that's a fine promise." My lips curled up at his words. "There's always later."

"I'll count on it," he said and slapped my ass, sending me out of the bathroom laughing.

Chapter 16

TO CALL THE New York City charity fashion show crowded was an understatement. I had no idea the place was going to be so huge and magnificent with so many beautiful people huddled together. Cameras blitzed everywhere, the flashes bright and blinding.

The thick red rug muffled the sound of my high heels as we ascended a flight of stairs to the entrance, past the ushers and what looked like hundreds of journalists that had been camping out for days.

As the cameras began to flash, Jett's arm went possessively around my waist, and I tensed, unsure where to look.

This was not the kind of life I grew up with. I knew for a fact that I'd never belong, no matter what I did and how much I tried.

Our mid-class little white house that had seen better days had been a far cry from the marble floors, designer dresses, and million-dollar diamonds around me.

"Mr. Mayfield. Jett!" someone yelled, and others followed suit.

"Who is she?"

"Are you dating?"

"Are you excited to watch the live fashion show?"

Someone shouted, "Look, she has a ring. Jett, are you engaged? When's the wedding?"

The crowd went berserk, the questions culminating in a crescendo—about me, about us.

Jett stopped, and his grip around my waist tightened as he turned, forcing me to face the hailstorm of flashing cameras. He didn't seem affected, or the least bit nervous. It seemed in every way as if he had done it dozens of times before, which he probably had, given that he was rich and, until recently, NYC's most eligible bachelor.

My heart stopped as he pulled me forward—toward the crowd of journalists.

"Jett, is this your new girlfriend?" A guy stretched out a microphone. As Jett cleared his voice all of a sudden everyone became quiet.

"Actually, we've been dating for some time," he said in a clear and loud voice that carried no shaking, no signs that he was nervous. He squeezed his arm around my waist possessively. "May I introduce you my fiancée, Brooke Stewart?"

"When did you propose?" someone shouted from the back of the crowd.

"November 25th." He smiled proudly.

"Today?" they asked in unison.

"That's correct." He flashed another gorgeous smile. "I couldn't wait any longer to take this stunning woman off the market." His words trigged out laughs in the crowed. To my bewilderment, Jett turned to me. "The truth is, it was love at first sight, and we're expecting our first child."

I put on the slightest hint of a smile and waited out the storm. More questions came, alternated with congratulations, and more questions, but Jett answered them all.

After what seemed like an eternity, Jett moved us along, and we continued our way to the lobby.

"See, it wasn't that bad, was it?" he whispered in my ear.

I nodded, feeling high from all the adrenaline. "I can't believe you told them. Now we'll be in the papers."

He laughed out loud as he turned to regard me. "That was the plan. You know, I cannot let you stay in the shadows forever. Or how else could I explain it if we're married by next week?"

My heart stopped. My whole body felt faint.

"You want to get married next week?" I asked in disbelief.

"Actually I want to get married this weekend. Just a small wedding, before we plan our big one. What do you think?" His words were casual, as if he were talking about the menu in a restaurant.

"Jett…I don't know what to say."

"What about, I love you?"

"You know I love you."

"Then marry me this weekend." He touched my cheek gently, heedless of the crowd that had begun to spill in around us. "Brooke, I don't want to wait any longer. I don't want to have the stress of planning a wedding while fearing you could change your mind and leave me at the altar."

I shook my head. "I would never do that."

"Yeah," Jett said, unconvinced. "So what do you say?"

"You know I would never say no."

***

It was slowly becoming packed as we weaved through the crowd.

Wherever I looked, more people arrived in stunning designer wear that probably cost a fortune. I even recognized some of those faces, adding names and movies.

There was the major with his wife and children, and then there were A-list celebrities. And then there was Grayson.

That's right.

Grayson.

I stopped, suddenly extremely surprised to see someone I knew.

He was standing to my right, sipping champagne as he talked with what looked like the tallest blond woman I had ever seen.

"Brooke?" Jett prompted, his voice jolting me out of my thoughts. Realizing that it might not be such a good idea to let Jett see me stare at another guy, I turned away, hiding my face with my hand, but it was too late.

Grayson's head turned to me, and our eyes connected across the short distance. As recognition dawned on him, his lips curled at the corners. He leaned forward, whispering something to the blonde, and before I knew it, he was heading for us.

Alone.

Damn.

"Oh, my God," I gasped.

It was too late to back out. But I had to try. If only I knew how?

Jett's hand on the small of my back became firm as he

guided me further into the crowd, toward Grayson, and for a split second, I pondered whether to just to turn around and dash for the exit, or let the inevitable take place and risk igniting Jett's extremely jealous nature.

When my gaze fell on the bar on the west side, an idea occurred to me.

"Jett!" I tugged at his sleeve to get his attention, the words gushing out of me in a nervous frenzy. "Can you get me a drink?" I smiled weakly as he looked at me. "I'm feeling awfully thirsty. In fact, if I don't get something to drink right now, I think I might black out."

Which wasn't even a lie. I couldn't deal with another discussion, or worse yet, another fight, and particularly not with one that was unjustified.

His face crumpled with worry. "Are you okay?"

I nodded unconvincingly. Behind Jett's shoulders, I watched Grayson forcing his way through the gathering crowds, stopping here and there to exchange a few words, but his gaze remained focused on us. If I didn't get rid of Jett right now, I'd have to introduce Grayson to him.

Think, Stewart. Think.

The modeling job had been a temporary thing to earn some money. But now, with the possibility of Jett being a murder suspect and me being officially engaged to one of the richest men in the world, I knew I couldn't return to it. Besides, I couldn't go back to the one place where I met

Gina. I wanted to move on, rather than risk being officially branded as an erotic model, and risk harming Jett's reputation along the way.

"I'm fine. It's nerves." I smiled weakly. Jett's frown deepened.

Did he *have* to be so uncanny in his ability to sense my emotional undercurrents?

"Relax," I said, infusing more confidence into my tone than I actually felt. "I've barely had any water today, and the one cup of coffee has made me a bit dizzy. I'm just a little bit dehydrated, so stop worrying all the time."

"I'll be back in a second." He pointed a finger to the marble floor beneath us. "You don't move from this spot. Okay?"

I scoffed and fought the urge to roll my eyes. "As if I'd go anywhere without you."

"I'm serious, Brooke."

"So am I." I motioned with my hand. "Come on."

Jett had barely turned his back on me, disappearing through the crowd, when Grayson reached me. A smile was still plastered on his face as he stepped in front of me, ignoring the crowd of people around us.

Dressed in a dark blue tailored suit with a matching gray tie, he looked more business like than I had ever seen him. Suddenly, my stomach filled with ice.

I didn't know the guy. I couldn't trust anyone. Because it

was too late to dash after Jett, I had to be careful around him.

Mustering the brightest and most confident smile I had, I waved at him. "Hi."

"Look who's here!" Grayson smiled again and leaned forward. For a moment, I thought he might be about to grab me in a bear hug or kiss my cheek. But he did neither of those.

I laughed nervously. "What can I say? It's a small world."

"I'm surprised to see you here."

"So am I." I shrugged, inwardly scolding myself for fostering the conversation. Grayson's gaze followed mine as I searched the crowd for Jett and spied him at the bar, towering over everyone else.

"I didn't realize you knew him," Grayson said, somewhat surprised.

"Who?" In my uncomfortable state, I didn't realize that he must have seen Jett and me together. My brows furrowed.

"Jett Mayfield." Grayson regarded me for a long moment, his smile vanishing. "I need to be frank, Jenna. I'm not happy about you dating my client."

My stomach flipped and my mind skidded to a halt as I eyed him, wondering if I had heard right.

"Client?" I asked carefully.

"Yes, client." He cocked his head, a disappointed scowl on his face. "Mr. Mayfield met up with me yesterday to discuss your work. He wants you to be exclusive to him, so he bought all your shots. An unusual request, I have to say, but then again, some of my clients like to think a girl belongs only to them. I call it something like a fixation."

My jaw dropped.

Jett had bought my pictures?

How the hell did he even know about them when I had only mentioned the job that morning?

Grayson probably misinterpreted my stunned silence because he continued, unfazed. "You could have so much going for you, Jenna. A client with a fixation on a pregnant woman's body is a rare gem. For your sake, I advise you keep a professional distance. That is, if you want more work and better pay. Otherwise, he'll lose interest before you know it, which would be bad for your future career."

For a few seconds, I just stood there, rooted to the spot, as his words sunk in.

Jett bought all of my pictures.

Not just one or two. But all, past and future.

"Actually, I don't think there's a need for that," I found myself saying. "I've decided to quit."

I raised my chin and took a deep breath. Grayson stared at me.

"Mr. Mayfield is a very influential man," Grayson

started. "Some of my models decide to go that route, taking on an offer that sounds like it would solve all their problems. He'll take care of you as long as—"

At my warning scowl, he trailed off, leaving the rest unspoken.

"He didn't pay me to quit, if that's what you're implying," I said dryly. "And for your information, Mr. Mayfield is my fiancé. I'm quitting for a different reason."

"Oh, I see." His gaze brushed over my strategically placed hand and the diamond ring sparkling in the lights. I could almost see the penny dropping. A short frown crossed his face, and his eyes narrowed, but it disappeared quickly. When he spoke again, his voice was soft, and concern was etched on his face.

"So, why? If you don't mind me asking."

Shrugging uncomfortably, I racked my mind for all the excuses I had come up with, but my mind remained surprisingly blank. There were too many to go into detail.

"I'm sorry," I said, deciding not to go into specifics.

"Don't apologize." He nodded knowingly, as though he might have expected it from me. "Gina's death was a blow to us all. I understand that, given the circumstances, you have changed your mind about working for me.

He thought I quit because of Gina.

That was only partially true, but I could live with that. I most certainly couldn't live with the implication that I might need a man to take care of me.

"Yeah." I crossed my arms over my chest, suppressing a shiver, and regarded him coolly. "I only knew her for a short time, but...I liked her. She was a good person."

For a brief second, melancholy flashed across his face. "She was," he said. "Well, take all the time you need. If you ever change your mind, I want you to know that you'll always be welcome to join my team again. No hard feelings."

I stared at him, my unease replaced by gratitude. "Thank you. I appreciate it."

Grayson smiled and then scanned the crowd. The blond woman waved at him, drawing his attention. If I wanted answers, I had to act now. He turned back to me, opening his mouth.

"Did they find out who did it?" I asked before he could excuse himself.

"Not yet," he said. "I'm still waiting for the detective to answer my calls. I guess it's still early in the investigation."

I frowned, suddenly interested. "Why's that?"

"He never finished questioning everyone. After you left, he made a call and had to leave. Call of duty, or so he said. I'm still waiting on an update."

My heart pounded harder.

Grayson wasn't involved. He didn't know more than I did. His confusion made it pretty clear.

Whoever the detective was, he might have followed me, which would explain the rap at the door in the middle of the night and the letter.

"Are you okay, Jenna?" Grayson asked.

"Yeah." I smiled at him. "It was good to see you, Grayson."

He stretched out his hand, and I took it to shake it. "Goodbye, Jenna. It was good to see you, too."

And then he left, his words echoing in my mind long after he was gone.

Chapter 17

"HI, BABY." JETT'S lips, soft and hot, brushed my skin as he returned from the bar. "Sorry it took so long."

I turned to him, mustering up a grin. "I thought you got lost."

"Well, I *got* lost," he whispered against my skin. "But not here. Somewhere in a place that's dark and much more soft."

I slapped his upper arm playfully, marveling at the firmness of his triceps. Holy shit, was it my imagination, but did his muscles feel larger and harder?

"Does this mysterious place happen to start with a V?"

"No, baby. It's your heart." He kissed my cheek, then

my neck, and came to hover at my ear. "The day I fell in love with you, I got lost in the rhythm of your heartbeat. It's safe to say I still haven't found a way out, and I doubt I ever will." He held up his hand. "That's not to say the V place isn't a favorite of mine as well. In fact, it's my number one trip."

God, the slightest hint at sex made my heart flutter and my core quiver.

He passed me a drink. "I got you freshly pressed orange juice."

"Thank you," and took the glass out of his hand. I took a sip, then another, realizing that not only was I thirsty, but the baby inside me was demanding food. It felt as though I hadn't stopped eating since finding out I was pregnant.

But food had to wait.

"Jett?" I turned to him, eyeing him. "The strangest thing happened when you were gone. I met Grayson."

"Who?" His green eyes turned a shade darker as he cocked his head.

"Grayson," I repeated, taking another sip. "You know, my ex boss."

"Right." He paused shortly, his gaze probing mine. Probably to assess if it had been a good idea to leave me all alone. "Where is he?"

"Oh, he left." I smiled at him. "He's a busy photographer."

His eyes narrowed, and his lips curved down. "So I gather you talked?"

"Yes."

"About what?"

Even though his face remained expressionless, I could detect the hint of mistrust and the streak of jealousy that always seemed to make me wary of any man who so much as looked at me.

My heart fluttered. Even though jealousy wasn't a good thing in a relationship, I loved it about Jett.

"Don't worry. Nothing special. I told him I couldn't do the job anymore, that I quit."

"That's all?" He sounded so genuinely relieved I felt like laughing.

"Yep, that's all." My lips twitched involuntarily. "Except...come to think of it, he mentioned something quite interesting." I cocked my head and watched his reaction.

My implication had the desired the effect.

Jett's eyes went a shade darker and he froze. For the first time ever I had him muffled. I stepped toward him and wrapped my arms around his waist. To the others, it probably looked like I was hugging him, but I just wanted him to close to me.

"He told me that you bought my pictures. But the way I see it, that's not possible because that would imply that you've been spying on me." I gave a short laugh as my fingers traveled up his chest and settled on that one special place where his heart was located. "Right, Jett?"

His nervousness disappeared instantly, and his lips curved into a nonchalant smile, matching my grin. "Well, I might or might not be the owner of a very fine collection."

I stared at him.

Was it all just a figment of my imagination or was Jett proud of it?

"So you admit it?" I frowned.

"Do you want me to lie?" He cocked his head, amusement flaring in his eyes. "In my defense, you're really good. I would never have pegged you for a pin up girl, but, fuck—" he made a whistling sound "—you know how to turn me on."

I dropped my hands before people began to stare. "Is that your way of saying that I shouldn't have quit?"

"No." He pulled me back to him but not too close. "It's my way of saying that you're too good to be in that kind of job. And I'll admit—" he let out an exaggerated sigh "—I cannot stand other people jerking off over your pics. If Grayson hadn't agreed to our deal, I would have tracked down every guy who owned a copy and cut off their dicks."

I let out a nervous laugh. "You wouldn't have."

"I would have." He gritted his teeth. "It was bad enough that Kenny stared at you."

I smiled. "You don't strike me as a jealous person, Mayfield."

He adjusted his tie. "I'm not jealous, I'm just protecting what is mine."

Seriously?

"You have no reason to be jealous," I said.

"I know that, but it is the thought of losing you to another man that's unbearable."

"Jett?" I placed a finger on his sexy lips, muffling his words. "You won't." In that moment, the crackle of a microphone was replaced by an announcement. "I think the show's about to start."

"Ready to take our seats?" Jett asked.

"Is there going to be food?" I joked.

"After the show, I'm taking you out for dinner," he said and kissed my forehead. "Come on, baby."

I sighed inwardly and followed Jett to the row of seats overlooking the entire runway. He motioned at the chairs with our names, and I sat down, food forgotten as I stared at the magnificent display before my eyes.

The runway had been set up to look like a bridge over water and was illuminated by a complex lighting design with the lights shifting, magnifying, and fading at various intervals. I had never seen anything like it, but then again, I had never attended a fashion show, and most certainly not something as elaborate and expensive as this.

I had barely taken my seat when arms wrapped around me, and a familiar voice almost shrieked in my ear. It almost sounded like…

"Sylvie." I jumped up in surprise.

"Surprise." She slumped onto the chair next to me with her usual grace and regarded me and Jett for a long moment, her eyes sparkling. "Congrats on getting engaged. That's like the best news ever. I was so happy when I heard you two were tying the knot."

Jett's eyebrows rose in surprise a moment before he erupted in laughter.

"Okay." Sylvie shrugged and rolled her eyes. "At first, I was like, 'run, run the hell faster,' but after I heard about the ring part, I was like, 'hey, that's a pretty good deal.' But seriously, I wish you guys nothing but the best. By the way, you look stunning."

"So do you." I blinked in succession, then looked from her to Jett and back to her. "What are you doing here?"

"I invited her," Jett said, amused. "You gals deserve a bit of fun. Given that this is your thing"—he pointed around him with the enthusiasm of a sleeping pill—"I thought I might use my social influence to get you one of the best seats here."

"Thank you," I whispered. My stomach churned again when I spied a waiter carrying trays filled with champagne flutes and what looked like mouthwateringly delicious things to nibble on. And he looked like he was heading for us. Or at least in our direction.

"Oh, I want one of those," I said before I could stop myself.

Jett laughed, the buzz of his cell phone interrupting the sound I had grown to love so much.

"Oh shit. It's work," he mouthed. "I have to take this. Be right back." He stood and waved his cell at me. I nodded, my attention focused on the waiter as he approached us. I declined the champagne but grabbed a few tiny, salty bites that would have to do until I could get my hands on real food.

"I'm so happy we're here," Sylvie said the moment he was gone.

"Me too."

"He's holding a secret engagement party tomorrow," Sylvie said the moment he was gone.

I turned to her. "How do you know?"

"Kenny told me."

"Aren't you supposed to keep it a secret?"

"I'm your best friend. Of course I have to tell you. And I should tell you too that Jett included a note with the question if I wanted to be your maid of honor. Maybe he's not so bad after all. Not only did he get us in, he also paid for the dress."

Given Jett and Sylvie's history, I sensed that was about

the greatest compliment he could get.

I took a bite of the delicious thingy in my hand and regarded the silvery sheath enveloping her from head to toe. It was beautiful and probably very expensive. Jett had definitely splurged, and while I wasn't a fan of wasting money, the fact that he was trying to get on well with Sylvie pleased me. They were the most important people in my life, and I wanted them both to be around when the baby was born.

"I'm sure you'll cut him some slack in the future," I said jokingly.

"Depends on the way he treats you." Sylvie's gaze brushed my ring finger, and I held it up, fighting the urge to giggle, do a happy dance, or worse. I decided to save that for some other time, when we were alone, far away from the prying eyes of the paparazzi and their flashing cameras.

Sylvie gasped and then grabbed my hand, making a loud surprised sound that had a few people turning their head. "It's beautiful. Princess cut. Perfect in every way. I so want one of those."

"You'll get one eventually. Just wait and see." I smiled at her, wondering whether to ask the one question I knew would either make or break Sylvie's evening. In the end, mentioning a guy's name wasn't worth it.

"I can't believe you had no idea he was going to propose," Sylvie said. "So romantic."

She didn't know the half of it.

"The fight preceding Jett's proposal was anything but romantic, to be honest." Heat rushed to my face as I pictured Jett's sexy body. "It was very sexy, and very bare if you get my drift. He really stripped down."

Literally.

I blushed again.

"It doesn't matter as long as you have this little baby to show off." She laughed when the lights began to go off one by one and people flooded in to take their seats.

"I think the show's starting," I said, trying not to gawk at all the celebrities around us. "Where's Jett?"

Sylvie shrugged. "Probably hiding to avoid this. You know how men are."

"Yeah, but he wanted to be here."

I pulled out my cell phone and dialed his number. He replied at the second ring.

"Where are you?" I whispered.

"Babe—" A slight pause. His voice sounded strained. A honk sounded off somewhere. Was there traffic noise in the background? "You know that's not really my thing. Catch you in ten minutes when the show's over?"

The show was going to last more than ten minutes.

He was bailing on me.

"What? No!"

"Sylvie's there. I'm sure she'll be great company," Jett

said. "After the show's over, I'm going to take you both out on dinner. Love you."

And with that, he hung up. I stared at the phone incredulously, then peered at Sylvie.

"What did you expect?" She rolled her eyes. "I bet Kenny persuaded him to go for drinks, and Jett jumped in wholeheartedly. Probably didn't even need much persuasion."

"Wait. Kenny's here?"

She nodded, confusion crossing her face. "Yeah, how else do you think I got here?"

For some reason, Brian's words popped into my mind. He had been secretive, strange even.

He's a good guy, but he's extremely revengeful. So when he says he'll deal with a situation, I usually choose to believe he'll do just that. He's been saying that for weeks.

Combine that with the fact that his partner in crime was here, it was the perfect recipe for trouble.

Something didn't add up.

Coupled with the fact that Jett had gone to so much trouble to get us in, buy both Sylvie and me dresses, even though he hated anything fashion related, didn't sit well with me.

And then Kenny was here as well. Jett hadn't even mentioned him.

"Call me suspicious, but I think they're trying to get rid

of us." I raised my brows at Sylvie.

"What do you mean?"

I sighed. "Brian said something strange."

"Hey," a woman behind us said. "We're trying to watch this."

"Sorry," Sylvie mouthed to her, then turned back to me, in a quieter voice "You're going to listen to that guy?"

"I have no choice." I shrugged. "Something is up. We have to go."

She shot me a panicked look, probably fearing my next words.

"Grab your handbag," I said and stood. "Come on."

"I saw that one coming." She heaved an annoyed sigh. "Stewart, I swear I'll make you watch Jason Statham movies on replay for the rest of your life if you drag my ass out of here without a very good reason."

A viable threat.

Jason Statham movies were the stuff of my nightmares. Under different circumstances, I would have probably thought twice, but not today.

"I think I heard traffic noise in the background." Ignoring her, I dashed through the crowd, heading outside.

The fact that we were heading in the wrong direction slowed us down, but eventually we reached the red carpet and the parked taxis.

"Where is he?" I mumbled, scanning the busy street.

There were people everywhere.

It took me a while to spy the striking black sports ride with its tinted windows stuck in traffic. I had seen it so many times that I would have recognized it anywhere.

"There's Kenny," Sylvie almost screamed. "Hey—"

I clamped a hand over her mouth. "Are you crazy? You can't draw their attention to us." I scanned the street for Jett and spied him standing next to Kenny.

They exchanged words, and then they got into his car.

"What are they doing?" I asked and grabbed Sylvie's hand, dragging her behind me, both balancing on high heels and shivering in our evening gowns.

"You can't possibly be serious," Sylvie protested, but that didn't slow me down. "I don't know how you can walk in this dress."

"Call it a necessity."

"More like stalking your guy." Sylvie let out a laugh.

"Oh, shut up." I set my jaw and tightened my grip around her hand so I wouldn't lose her in the crowd.

Why hadn't Jett said anything about leaving? And where the heck were they going? As we reached the road, the traffic lights changed and Kenny's car began to move out of the parking lot.

Fuck!

They were about to drive away.

In that instant, a taxi stopped a few inches from us and a

couple got out. I raised my hand, hailing it before it could speed off.

"Don't lose the black sports car," I instructed the driver and settled in the backseat with Sylvie, my gaze fixed on the road ahead.

My heart raced so hard I was sure it would burst out of my chest.

Even Sylvie seemed nervous. Her hand wrapped around mine and she gave it a light squeeze. "This is so exciting."

Okay, maybe not nervous.

But then she didn't know about Gina and the letter.

"Where do you think they're going?" Sylvie whispered, her own suspicion finally piqued.

"No clue, but I guess we'll find out soon enough," I muttered.

Chapter 18

WE DROVE FOR a long time, more because of the heavy traffic rather than because of the distance, before we reached the Manhattan coastline along the Hudson River. Kenny's car took a sharp turn and stopped in the distance, killing the taillights. We parked at a safe distance, far enough away that they wouldn't notice us, but close enough that we'd be able to follow if they left.

"Isn't that the North Cove marina?" Sylvie said.

"I think so. What are they doing here?"

Sylvie shrugged her shoulders. "No idea. Maybe enjoying the view?"

"Maybe," I said, unconvinced.

In the distance, I could see the yachts floating at docks scattered along the river, their decadent lights casting golden reflections on the dark water. Sylvie must have noticed the same.

"Maybe Jett owns a boat and Kenny wants to check it out. You know how men are," Sylvie whispered even though no one could hear us.

Straining my brain, I tried to remember whether Jett had mentioned owning a yacht there. I didn't think so but that didn't mean he might not.

He owned one back in Italy.

"Or maybe they're just hanging out."

"This late when they could go to a bar?" Sylvie whispered.

"You're right," I muttered.

"Are you getting out?" the driver asked.

I peered at the car ahead.

"Not yet," I said. "Just wait."

The driver huffed and began to busy himself with his cell phone, which was fine by me.

We sat in silence for at least ten minutes, then another ten. When nothing happened, I breathed out a sigh of annoyance. The sports car was bathed in darkness. Even if it weren't for the safe distance, the tinted glass made seeing inside impossible.

What the fuck were they doing in there? Were they even

still in the car?

Both my curiosity and suspicion were killing me. I had to know, not least because Jett had promised no more secrets.

I exchanged a glance with Sylvie.

"You know," she whispered so the driver wouldn't hear us, "this kind of reminds me of those movies where they meet with a drug lord, or they do an exchange of some sort. If you get the meaning."

"You're being silly."

My blood froze in my veins. What if she was right?

"We're going to have a look," I said to the driver after paying and making sure to tip him generously. "Can you pick us up in ten minutes?"

"You sure that's a good idea?" Sylvie asked when the driver took off.

"Something isn't right." I peered at Kenny's car again. "I want to talk to them and find out who they're waiting for."

"Is this really a good idea?" Sylvie repeated, then yanked at my arm, pulling me down. "Look. They're getting out."

I peered over her shoulder. Sure enough, Kenny and Jett had exited and rounded the car, and were now sitting on the hood, watching the coast.

"I don't like this," I whispered. "Come on. I need to talk to Jett."

We had barely moved from the spot when a deafening

bang echoed through the night, followed by two more. They sounded like gunshots, only much louder.

Fire lit up the sky in the distance.

My heart stopped, and a quiet scream escaped my throat.

Flickering orange flames rose above the water, ascending into a spiral of smoke.

"Holy shit. A yacht exploded," Sylvie uttered in shock.

The fire flared brighter, and yet I couldn't move. I couldn't talk or do anything. The fire was so bright I was sure it could be seen for miles.

"Oh, my god," I whispered as realization dawned on me.

Jett had something to do with it.

As if sensing my thoughts, Jett turned. I thought I saw surprise and disbelief washing over his face, though I couldn't be sure that he had glimpsed me in the darkness.

Had he seen me?

But there was no time to talk because the taxi pulled up next to us.

The driver opened the passenger door and called out, "Hey, missus. Pack it up. Let's go."

Whatever was going on, he obviously didn't want to get involved. No one would be paying him for answering the police's questions all night.

I nodded my head but didn't budge from the spot. The

taillights of Kenny's car glimmered to life and then sped off.

I turned to Sylvie and found her staring at me, confusion reflecting in her face.

"Hey!" the driver called out, his voice carrying enough annoyance to make me flinch.

Sylvie straightened and helped me up. We slumped onto the backseat, and the driver took off without so much as a glance back. As we drove back to the fashion show, I couldn't help but wonder whose yacht had caught fire and why the heck it happened while Kenny and Jett had been camped out not far away.

And most importantly, what had Jett done?

Brian's words echoed through my mind:

Knowing Jett, it doesn't take long for him to jump the gun. When he's hell-bent on doing something, he really gets it in his head, even if it's a bad idea. It wouldn't really be that much of a surprise.

Chapter 19

THE NEWS ABOUT the explosion was splashed all over the newspapers and CNN the next day and the days after. It wasn't so much the yacht that made the headlines but the media's fascination with two men.

Sitting at the kitchen table, I went over each and every article. The headlines read:

SUSPECTED HUMAN TRAFFICKING GANG LEADER JONATHAN MAYFIELD FLEES PRISON

MYSTERIOUS GUNFIRE RESULTS IN DEATH OF FIVE MEN

JONATHAN   MAYFIELD   DEAD   AFTER
SPECTACULAR ESCAPE FROM PRISON

PREVIOUSLY   UNDISCOVERED   BODIES
FOUND, ONE OF THEM HUMAN TRAFFICKING
GANG LEADER JONATHAN MAYFIELD

DRUG RING RESPONSIBLE FOR DEATH OF
REAL ESTATE MOGUL JONATHAN MAYFIED

"Are you still reading this?" Warm lips brushed my
earlobe.

A week had passed, but we still hadn't talked about *that*
day.

After Sylvie and I had returned to the charity event, we
tried our best to remain unaffected, pretending to be
clueless, and it worked. As the best friend she was, I didn't
even have to ask her to keep quiet. She understood. When
Jett returned to the show a few minutes after me, he acted
like nothing had happened. We had dinner, then joined the
engagement party he had planned for us.

Everything was fine.

A perfect façade.

Everyone had believed us.

But today was different.

I still had to know. The excuses I had made for not

asking were torturing me.

I turned around, facing him. He leaned against the table, a coffee cup in his hand as he watched me. "Jett, I saw you that day."

His eyes remained pinned on me, but he said nothing.

"If you're involved, you don't have to tell me. But just answer this: did you help Nate escape?"

It was the only reasonable explanation I could draw from the newspaper articles. The past few days I hadn't dared to ask him, but I could no longer keep quiet because I was sure that my assumption was right.

"Brooke…" Jett let out an exaggerated sigh and put his cup down.

"Did you get him that boat?" I persisted.

Jett continued to stare at me, his beautiful face dark and mysterious.

"Baby, you worry too much." His arms wrapped around my waist, drawing me close to him. "My biggest fear isn't you leaving me, like your father did your mother, but losing you due to circumstances out of my control. Since the day of your kidnapping, I promised myself that I'd keep you safe, no matter what. Whether you want it or not, I'll always care for you and protect you. That Nate's dead is unfortunate, but I won't shed a tear for a man who killed hundreds. A man who wanted you dead."

"You still haven't answered my question. You visited

him in prison, didn't you? " He sighed again. I eyed him curiously. "You helped him escape? Come on, Jett. Tell me. I know you knew the boat would explode. Like I said, I saw you that day."

He brushed a strand of hair out of my face.

"I will only say this." Jett's smile disappeared. "He was stupid to trust the wrong people."

His eyes glimmered, and something flashed across his face.

Pride.

"You mean…"

"Yes." He nodded. "He trusted someone to get him out."

Now I understood.

Jett had lied to Nate.

All his visits to prison had been a means to build the trust, to get the plan moving. He didn't have to tell me.

"I had been planning this for a long time. Brian told me not to do it, but I couldn't, Brooke." He shrugged. "Nate would never have stopped. Because of him, your friend's dead. Who would have been next? You? I couldn't take the risk."

He was right.

My thoughts racing, I sat down, unable to wrap my mind around the fact that Jett had carefully hid everything from me. "But…how did you do it?"

He smiled, his thumb stroking my cheek. "Well, let's just say don't ever underestimate your people. If you're not careful enough, they might start working for someone else. In Nate's case it was Danny. Like I said before, everyone has a price."

My heart skipped a beat.

"Danny? You found him?"

"Yes. It wasn't even hard. All we had to do was track down Nate's suppliers and dealers, then track their calls and locations for a few days. Danny was the only one to come near you and Gina. Turned out he had been watching you for weeks."

The words lingered in the air, their magnitude weighing down on me.

My eyes widened. "You're saying…" I trailed off, unable to speak out the obvious.

"Yes." Jett nodded again. "He killed your friend and followed Nate's orders to frame me. We have enough proof from his phone conversations. Everything points to him." He took a deep breath and let it out slowly. "I guess he couldn't stay away from you."

"Oh, my God." I leaned back, frowning.

"Danny's dead," Jett said softly.

I looked up and found his expression serious. "But there was no mention of him."

"In there?" Jett grabbed a paper. My eyes followed his

finger, as it hovered over the words 'undiscovered bodies found.' "He got what he deserved. It was long overdue. The police are going to charge Danny's cousin, Barrow, with Gina's murder. The weapon and photos were found at his place."

"I still don't understand." I shook my head. "I told you about Gina the day of the explosion; how did you know that fast that it was Danny?"

"I didn't," Jett said. "It was luck. We only found out during the police investigation. It's a good thing he's dead."

Moisture gathered in my eyes. I lifted my hand to wipe away my unshed tears, but Jett beat me to it. His thumb stroked my cheek gently, the soothing motion touching my heart.

"I'm not sad." My voice was hoarse, croaky.

"I know."

"It's just…" Another tear trickled down my cheek. At least I wasn't sobbing. "I can't believe you found him. I can't believe you found the guy who killed my sister. Ten years. That's how long I waited for justice. And now I can't believe it's over."

Jett kneeled before me, his hand touching mine. "Only the bad part, Brooke. The good part, which is us, will never be over."

Epilogue

Fifteen months later

THERE ARE SO many kinds of loves, but only one kind—true love—can change a person and raise that person to a meaningful existence. Love is a beautiful thing. Sacred. It's the only feeling that can grow if you pay it enough attention and care for it. It's also the only thing that can give you more meaning than all material belongings.

I was sitting in the backseat with my eyes blindfolded, my leg brushing against Jett's at every turn, as the black limousine took us to a place God only knew.

Jett had made a big secret out of our destination so, naturally, the suspense was killing me.

"We have one hour before we need to get back to Treasure. Can you guess what my surprise is?" Jett said, his deep voice with the slightest hint of a Southern accent caressing my senses, and helped me out of the limousine.

"No." I smiled. "But I wish I could. You know how much I hate surprises."

He let out a pleased laugh. "But this one, I think, you'll love."

"You think? What happened to your usual, 'It will blow your mind'?"

"Well, this is different." He touched the small of my back to guide me forward. I could feel the wind on my skin. The air tasted salty. The cries of seagulls intermingled with the sound of waves crashing against a shore.

I had no idea where we were, but I liked it a lot.

Jett always made the best surprises. His inventiveness never failed to amaze me.

Finally, he removed the blindfold. I blinked once, twice, then took in the shore before me. The sun was shining and the sky was streaked with red and orange.

No surprise there.

Jett beamed at me. "Now turn around." He touched my shoulder and motioned for me to follow his command. I did as he said. My smile vanished. My whole being froze.

I recognized the setting and its private beach immediately. We were standing in the backyard of a place we once visited. It been a long time ago, but even back then I knew I'd never forget it.

Countless rose petals were scattered across the trail in the sand, forming a path illuminated by candles lit to either side. They were leading to a sandcastle. I walked toward it, my heart beating frantically as I tried to process what was happening. As I reached it, I spied a key with a note attached to it. The note read:

HOME.

A small arrow pointed ahead. At Jett's silent encouragement, I followed it until I glimpsed the front door.

"Jett." My voice reflected my excitement. "You can't be serious."

"Very serious here." His fingers intertwined with mine, and he spun me around. "The moment I realized you liked this house, I knew it would be perfect for us, so I had to get it. It wasn't easy. The previous owner had changed her mind about selling it, so it took me months to convince her to sell it to us." He pulled me forward gently but with enough persuasion to make me follow. "Come on. Treasure's waiting for us."

I was so shocked, I couldn't reply. Thankfully, my legs

began to move, following Jett up the trail.

With shaky fingers I unlocked the door.

"Mama." Treasure's voice echoed through the hall as she dashed for me, the smiling nanny behind her forgotten. I scooped her up and kissed her, burying my nose in her hair to inhale her scent.

She had grown so quickly.

With her black hair and beautiful face, she was in every way a carbon copy of Jett.

"Dada." She stretched her hand out to Jett, and I let him take her, instantly catching the glint of adoration in his eyes as we returned outside into the balmy breeze.

With the warm sunlight on my face, I closed my eyes to the sound of little Treasure giggling as her dad held her up in the air and spun her in circles—the sound of the two even more calming and beautiful than the realization that we were a family in our family home.

We were free to be happy.

Right before returning to NYC, we had spent a few months in Bellagio. It had become something like a second home to us. We were finally free to live the life we'd always envisioned without a threat hanging over our heads.

The news of Nate's yacht blowing up had broken less than twelve hours after the explosion. Officially, no one knew what exactly happened that fateful night a year and a half ago, but I knew for a fact that Kenny and Jett had been involved. Jett seemed more carefree, as though all his worries had lifted off his shoulders.

Had he singlehandedly orchestrated Nate and Danny's death?

Based on his words, probably. But we never talked about it again since the 'talk.' And to be honest, I didn't want to know every detail.

Jett had or hadn't done what he had deemed necessary to protect his family, and that was it. He got rid of my demons. I owed him my life and my happiness.

For a long time, I had wondered what to do with the estate I had inherited from Alessandro Lucazzone. After Treasure was born, Jett came up with the idea of turning it into a charity. A home for abused women—an idea which appealed to me on a very deep level. It was the solution I had been searching for, and so he assigned one of his best account managers the task of transforming the Lucazzone estate, which had been a place of abuse for far too many years, into a safe haven for those who needed to learn how to feel safe again.

At some point, Jett's dad had woken up from his coma. Jett had yet to forgive him, but Treasure's birth had mellowed him down a bit. An improvement in their relationship didn't seem so far-fetched after all. Besides, I was working hard to make it happen.

As for Jett and I, we had tied the knot twice: the first

time in a private little ceremony in Las Vegas, and the second time in a big and beautiful ceremony in Italy only a few months ago, after which we had taken a much-deserved vacation.

Jett's urgency to work on baby number two couldn't wait.

Apparently, he wanted an entire football team.

He joined me in a few steps, and together we watched Treasure playing in the sand, her nanny nearby.

"Lots of fond memories here." Jett smiled, his gaze hazing as he thought back to a very naughty day we had spent in the house. At that time, I had thought Jett had broken in.

Turned out he was an amazing actor.

"The best," I said.

I turned my head to him because I couldn't believe my luck. This insanely gorgeous man...I knew I would love him forever.

I thought back to the first day I met him two and a half years ago. The way I had snatched my umbrella from his grip and sped off, because he had seemed intense and arrogant. I knew now that I hadn't meant to run away from him. I had been running from myself in fear of unleashing something inside of me that could destroy me. If he hadn't come after me and hired me for a position in his company without my knowing, we might never have ended up together.

"You got one thing wrong," I said when he joined me. "It was your inflated ego that made me want you in the first place, not your stubbornness."

He raised a brow. "Not the fact that you thought I was hot?"

I shook my head in a weak attempt to stop his ego from growing to immense proportions.

Yes, I had thought he was hot.

Yes, I wanted to jump into bed with him.

But his confidence could convince even a bear to give up his prey.

"I couldn't stand you because I knew I could easily be yours. It was all too easy to run and lie to myself that I wanted you but didn't need you. However, the truth was, I wanted you because I needed you in some way. I just didn't want to be *that* woman who got weak, only to be used and discarded."

"You're not that woman, because I'm not that kind of guy." He took my hands in his. "I like you needing me, Brooke. It makes me feel wanted. It makes me want to see you happy. I wish you'd ask for more so I could give you all that I have."

"I'm already demanding," I said.

Jett shook his head. "No. Not to me, you're not. You should be *more* demanding. I love it when you ask for more, especially when I'm inside of you. I love it when you scream."

Heat rushed to my face. "I don't scream."

"The times you do it fuels my imagination." He glanced at me softly, his green eyes shimmering with happiness. "Since you're married to me and all, I can ask for anything," Jett continued. "So this is what I want. I'm asking for your promise."

"What promise?"

"That you'll stay with me forever."

I shook my head. "I thought you forgot about it."

He let out a laugh. "Fat chance. I've already married you, haven't I? Now it's only fair that you return the favor."

"You play dirty."

"That's one of the things you love about me." He grinned. "You should be grateful for the fact that I'm asking. I could force you—" he raised his eyebrows "—but I won't, because I'm a gentleman."

I snorted. "You're no gentleman."

"I'm not?" He pressed his hand against his chest. "Now I'm hurt."

I laughed at his exaggerated expression. "You're more manipulative than an insurance sales guy. Sweet-talking is worse than forcing. With forcing, you sort of see it coming. With manipulation, you're being played."

"Are you trying to tell me my charm's working on you?"

The seriousness in his eyes made me conclude that beneath our playful façade, he was still waiting for my promise. He had made his, and it was my turn.

"Okay," I said slowly. "I promise I won't leave you. I'll stay as long as you love me."

"Which means for a long time. Maybe even forever—depending on how much sex I get tonight."

"*Right.*" I bit my lip, trying hard not to laugh. In the end, it didn't work and I let out a snort. "Just to be clear, your charm's the only thing working its magic on me. You could never ever force me." I leaned my back against him and let him wrap his arms around me. Snuggled against his warm chest, I relaxed.

"You sure? 'Cause I could swear my charm's not the only thing that worked today. I could remind you of—"

I pressed my hand against his mouth because I knew exactly what he was about to say. He was getting out of control, and before we knew it, we'd be back in bed.

Or on the floor.

Against the wall.

I cringed at the direction my thoughts were taking.

Jett removed my hand gently, finishing his statement. "—all the ways I made you come without employing force."

"No need," I said, slightly breathless.

"You're right. Why waste time talking?"

I squealed as he pulled me down on the sand and pushed himself on top of me, burying me under his weight. Time seemed to stand still for a moment. And then he smiled—that beautiful smile of his that always made me wonder what it'd be like to melt with him forever. Above him, the stars were beginning to show—beautiful like a canvas—and yet they couldn't take away from Jett's magnificence.

Yes, Jett Mayfield was perfect. Complicated but still perfect.

Perfect with all his faults and imperfections.

My relationship—even with all the fighting, the arguing, and the effort we put in—was all worth it.

And so I pray our love story will never end.

The End

If you liked this book, please consider leaving a review.

I'm a writer of happy endings, and if you like this final book in the No Exceptions series, you might also enjoy

AN INDECENT

PROPOSAL:

THE INTERVIEW

BY J.C. REED AND JACKIE STEELE

"It was supposed to be easy. Hire a professional actor to play my fake fiancé. But when he steps in front of my door to pick me up for The Interview, my heart stops. Chase Wright is perfect. And hot. I mean like, burn up your dress hot. However, Chase isn't professional at all. I hate what he does to me with his sinfully sexy blue eyes. I hate that he wants me in his bed.

One month...that's all I need him for. All I have to do is stay out of his bed.

But the rules slowly begin to change. My fake fiancé suddenly becomes my fake husband. When Chase offers me an indecent proposal, it's too late to fire him. It's too late to decline.

Never miss a release.

As a subscriber, you'll also receive an email reminder on release day:

http://www.jcreedauthor.blogspot.com/p/mailing-list.html

AN INDECENT PROPOSAL: THE INTERVIEW
BY J.C. REED & JACKIE STEELE

PREVIEW

I needed a husband—and fast. Not literally, of course. Just for the weekend, or as long as my stepfather would be in town. A relationship was the excuse I had given for not visiting Waterfront Shore for the last three years. Three years of running away from the place of my dreams and nightmares, and a past better left buried forever. And now my lie was catching up with me, because there was no husband or fiancé in sight, not even a boyfriend or a date to play the part.

"Hire an actor," said Jude, who was looking up from her computer screen. "In fact, he's perfect." She jumped up and headed over to me, her chiffon dress revealing long, tanned legs as she sat down on the sofa and tucked her legs beneath her. I stared open-mouthed at the half-naked model on the screen. He looked hot, no doubt about it, but he also looked—

"Desperate," I mumbled to myself.

"I wouldn't exactly call you 'desperate.' More like 'inventive' or—"

"Thanks," I muttered, cutting her off. "But I was talking about the guy."

For a moment we remained silent as I read the text beneath the picture of a man with a strong chin, dark brown hair, and eyes the color of an ocean shimmering in the sunlight, a shade of eye color I'd never seen before. I figured it was either Photoshopped, or they were contact lenses, which only managed to fortify my first impression of him.

Desperate. Plain desperate.

And his description in his own words didn't help improve his image, either.

Chase is a very nice, humorous, and down-to-earth lover of female beauty. He knows how to cook and offers to carry things when shopping.

"He sounds dreamy," Jude gushed.

I fought the urge to roll my eyes at her. "He sounds like a bellboy with playboy aspirations. Either that, or he's a crook waiting for gullible women to fall for his creepy charm. I bet the profile's fake."

PROLOGUE

Out of all the dates in my life, Tuesday at 10 a.m. was about the worst time disaster could strike. I was sitting in the waiting area of LiveInvent Designs—the one place where I had been dying to get an interview since finishing college.

Apart from me, nineteen other graduates were waiting for their big chance, all dressed in immaculate, tailored business suits—the kind I couldn't afford. But what I couldn't offer in expensive clothes, I knew I could make up in hard work and dedication. I was a professional, and as such I was determined to make a good impression.

"Lauren Hanson?"

I straightened up in my seat and smiled as one of the personal assistants called my name. "Yes." I stood and took a deep breath, waiting for further instructions.

"Please take the elevator up to the thirtieth floor. Someone will be expecting you."

The thirtieth floor.

According to LiveInvent's website, it was the place where the big-shot strategists worked. Los Angeles wasn't just home to some of the greatest marketing companies in the United States; it was also the best place to get started and to experience an environment of "what if," not just "if only."

When I applied for a graduate position as a marketing assistant, I had never even considered the possibility that one of them might like my resume enough to want to meet me personally. But now it was happening.

My dream was coming true.

I brushed my hands over my gray skirt nervously and with measured steps made my way to the elevator area, ignoring the people ambling up and down the corridor in their immaculate expensive clothes, seemingly oblivious to the outside world. They were probably used to their simple yet sophisticated surroundings, with marble floors and beautiful peonies, and calla lilies arranged in crystal centerpieces. The walls were adorned with polished frames displaying awards and the company's most successful projects showcased like little trophies.

I stopped in front of the elevators, and sighed happily. This wasn't just any workplace—it was heaven. And I wanted to be a part of it. Whatever it took.

This was my dream.

It *had* to come true.

A bell chimed, and one of the three elevator doors opened, giving me a view of a small but tastefully decorated space. Soft music was playing in the background at a pleasant volume. As I stepped into the small elevator, I bumped into someone.

It happened so quickly: my CV folder slipped out of my

hands and dropped to the floor. I squatted to reach for the folder when I noticed the pair of black, expensive slacks. I raised my eyes slowly, taking in the custom suit. No, it wasn't so much the suit, but more the tall height, his black hair, his broad shoulders, the sexy male fragrance he was wearing, that drew my attention to him.

His Rolex suggested that he wasn't an applicant. Probably an executive.

Before I knew it, the bell chimed again. I rose to my feet quickly before the doors closed again.

I pressed the backlit button embossed with the number thirty. No need to check him out, not when I didn't know if he wasn't an interviewer. Getting the job was more important than checking out the next hot guy.

I turned my back on him, and mentally recollected my primed answers to possible interview questions.

Breathe in, breathe out.

This was it…my big chance.

All my life I had worked hard for this exact day. Just a few more seconds. And then I would give it all my best, because I just had to have this job.

There was no possibility, no other option, no what-ifs.

If I wanted to make it in the business world and get out of my outstanding debt, I had to go the extra mile. I was ready—more than ever because any other outcome wasn't an option.

My hands turned clammy from my increasing nervousness, and my mouth went a little dry. I was so absorbed in my thoughts that I didn't register that the elevator had stopped moving until a little shake told me something was up. I looked up from the floor, only to see we had stopped at the twenty-ninth floor, and the doors had remained closed.

Seriously? Did we *have* to stop one floor below my destination?

I raised my eyebrows when the guy behind me began to press the buttons on the control panel in an impatient manner. The music was gone, plunging us into eerie silence.

Frowning, I turned to face him, wondering what the heck was going on, but all I caught were blue eyes just before the bulbs started to flicker. The lights flashed once more, then switched off, bathing us in complete darkness.

"What the—" I heard him cussing, his deep voice filled with annoyance.

For a moment, I held my breath, my heart pounding in my chest as I waited for the lights to switch on again. A few seconds passed, which turned into minutes. And still there was no light, no movement—nothing to indicate we even were in an elevator.

I blinked in succession, blind in the pitch-black.

As my brain tried to make sense of the situation, countless thoughts began to race through my mind. How long would it take until people noticed there was a technical glitch and sent repairmen? How long were the interviews scheduled to take, and if I appeared late, would I get a second chance? And finally, how long would the oxygen last in such a confined space?

Just theoretically asking.

Not that we were going to be stuck for much longer. Or suffocate anytime soon, because that would be a worst-case scenario. But it would only be natural to know...just in case.

I wasn't claustrophobic—actually, far from it. But dark, enclosed spaces weren't exactly my favorite place to be. And particularly not those with no clear exit sign. The minutes continued to fly until I was sure we had been in there for at least twenty minutes. Or maybe it just felt that way.

I sighed impatiently.

"There must be an assistance button," I said as I let my fingers brush over the cold steel wall. My hand touched his, and an electric jolt ran through me. I pulled back nervously.

"Sorry," I whispered.

"No problem."

In the silence around us, I could hear his finger pressing buttons every other second, as if that would make someone hurry faster. At last, the stranger let out a frustrated sigh. Something rustled, followed by shuffling.

I narrowed my gaze to focus in the pitch darkness, but my vision didn't sharpen to allow me to see contours.

Nothing stood out.

I groaned and braced myself against the feeling of helplessness growing inside me. Not seeing anything while knowing there was no window or door I could open was already scary. Combine that with the fact that I had no idea if help was on its way, and the entire situation was turning into a nightmare scenario.

The guy was probably just as frustrated as I was, because I heard him shifting.

"What are you doing?" I asked as more rustling sounds carried over from the floor.

"Trying to find my cell." His voice came from beneath me, which made me figure at some point he must have kneeled down—or assumed a sitting position.

I wet my lips nervously.

A stranger was doing God only knew what at my feet. Now that made it hard to ignore him.

For a moment, I considered joining him, and then the word "cell" registered in my mind. Of course! A phone was the answer to my prayers.

"Shit. It's not here. I must have left it in the car." He exhaled another frustrated sigh. "Do you have yours?"

"Not on me." Which was kind of the truth. The day before, my handbag, together with my purse and cell phone, had been stolen. Lucky for me, my credit cards were maxed out to the limit, and my pre-paid cell had both a lock and no minutes, so the loss was minimal.

"Okay." His tone was surprisingly calm as he drew out the word. "Let's see if the emergency phone's working."

I jumped back as his hand reached over my chest, almost touching the thin fabric of my top.

"Hello?" he asked. Silence fell. Holding my breath, I strained to listen. The line remained dead. No voice, no white noise, nothing to indicate anyone had been alerted to our situation.

My heart began to thump hard against my ribcage, and a thin rivulet of sweat rolled down my back as realization kicked in that it might take a while before someone was alerted.

"Can you try again?" My voice came so thin and raspy, I knew I was close to having a panic attack.

"No point. Phone's not working. Reception's gone. We're stuck," the guy said, almost bored. No panic. No whining. Just cool composure with a hint of an annoyance, as if the entire situation was a mere inconvenience he experienced on a regular basis. Unlike me, he seemed to breathe just fine.

He sighed. "Let's hope they won't close off the elevator area for the rest of the day," he said to himself with...humor?

I swallowed hard.

If that was true, and we ended up stuck in there all day, we'd never last. We'd run out of oxygen and—

Come to think of it, didn't I read somewhere that people could die within two hours when stuck in a confined space? And hadn't we already been stuck for some time?

A sense of foreboding settled in the pit of my stomach.

Something was wrong. Very wrong. I could feel it in the oppressive silence and the fact that the stranger had stopped pressing buttons and rummaging through his pockets. The air was getting increasingly hot, making it hard to breathe. The rivulet turned into a layer of sweat covering my entire back as I tried to force oxygen into my lungs.

In that moment, a loud thud reverberated from the walls, followed by a short, faint shrill.

An alarm?

Oh, my god.

This wasn't some technical glitch. It was a real-life emergency. Something had happened. Something really bad. Faintly, I could hear hurried steps, some of them pounding, but none of them seemed to stop near the elevators. Everyone would forget about the two people stuck in the elevator, because they had more pressing issues to attend to—like saving themselves. The alarm continued to blare in the distance.

To my utter shock, a whimper escaped my throat as fear

consumed me.

"Oh, God." My voice came high-pitched, reflecting the dark thought that kept circling in my mind.

I'm going to die.

The thought hit me so hard a wave of dizziness rushed over me. But, at twenty-two, I was too young for my demise, particularly because I hadn't even started to live my life yet. I had struggled through college while amassing a vast student loan debt that had kept me strapped for cash for years.

How ironic would it be if the one job I had thought would be the answer to my prayers might just kill me?

The thought of being stuck in a confined space, missing the most important interview of my life while dying from oxygen depletion, was too much. Suddenly, my breathing quickened, and my pulse began to race hard and fast.

I realized the whizzing sound echoing in my ears wasn't a result of my frayed nerves but a noise coming out of my mouth.

"I think I'm having a panic attack," I whispered.

"We'll be all right," the guy said, and this time I noticed how smooth and deep his voice was.

Sexy, with the slightest hint of a rumble to it.

Maybe my other senses were sharpened in the darkness, or we were indeed running out of oxygen and my brain was slowly starting to play tricks on me, but in the confined space I could smell him clearly. Not just his aftershave, but *him*—the man who couldn't see me. The only person who would witness my untimely death.

"I'm not sure." I choked on my voice. "What if no one comes?"

"What's your name?" Sexy Voice said.

"Lauren, but everyone calls me Laurie," I whispered.

Something warm brushed my shoulder, instantly raising goose bumps across my arm, and trailed down my arm until it touched my hand. Strong fingers clasped around my hand and squeezed, not hard enough to hurt me, but the motion helped me regain some of my composure, and make me realize that I wasn't alone.

"Okay, Laurie. This is likely just a temporary glitch. You need to calm down."

I *was* calm, wasn't I?

I'd opened my mouth to tell him that when the air whizzed out of my lungs in a hot *swoosh*. It sounded like someone was whistling, and not in a pretty way. And there I had thought it was the sound of the elevator, when it had been me all along.

"I can't," I whispered. "I can't breathe. I feel like I'm choking."

To my dismay, I started shaking and my breathing came faster.

"You're hyperventilating," Sexy Voice said, increasing

the pressure of his grip. "I need you to breathe with me. Okay, Laurie?" He inhaled and exhaled deeply, his hot breath caressing my skin, and I realized just how close he was standing. Under normal circumstances, too close for comfort.

Only, these weren't normal circumstances.

Staring blindly ahead, I followed his instructions, inhaling with him, holding my breath, and then exhaling again.

"Are you feeling better?" he asked.

I shook my head, even though he couldn't see me, as tears pricked the corners of my eyes.

"We can't even call for help. If we're stuck in here for a whole day, we'll die," I whispered.

"No." His tone was sharp. Defiant. "People know we're in here. Security is calling for help this instant."

"You don't know that," I muttered.

"Trust me. I do."

I wanted to believe him so badly my whole body hurt from the effort. But, for some reason, his words rang empty and senseless. "People can die in elevators. I read about it last week."

"Not us. Not today." His hands began to rub up and down my arms, as though to soothe me, but the motion only managed to send a layer of ice down my spine.

For a while, we just stood there, rivulets of sweat

running down my spine. The whole space, as small as it was, had the temperature of a sauna.

"It's so hot," I whispered. "I really can't breathe."

"You can do it, Laurie. Focus on my voice. Focus on taking slow, deep breaths through your nose, and exhale through your mouth. That's all that matters now. Nothing else."

I forced more air into my lungs, but even though oxygen reached my brain, somehow it didn't have the desired calming effect on me. "The funny thing is, I'm not ready to die," I said weakly, squeezing his hands for support.

"You won't." His determined tone left no room for discussion. "Tell me something about yourself." He was trying to divert my attention from the situation at hand, only it didn't work. "Where do you live? What do you like doing in your free time?"

"There's nothing to tell. I'm boring."

A sexy little laugh, then, "I highly doubt that, Laurie. You sound like an interesting person."

In spite of myself, I smiled. He had no idea how wrong he was. "No, really. I'm a bore."

"Well, try me. I'm in no hurry."

Neither was I. We'd probably been stuck for more than two hours, and I needed a distraction.

"Laurie," he prompted, hesitating. Or maybe he was having trouble breathing as well. And then I noticed it: a slight shaking and vibrating of the walls. It stopped almost as quickly as it had started.

His hands let go of me. Clothes rustled, and something dropped to the floor with a muffled thud. Then his hands were back on me, his bare skin brushing mine in the process, his fingers holding mine.

I realized he must have taken off his jacket and rolled up his sleeves. The air was getting hot. It wasn't just my imagination. Suddenly, I had a vision of dying without clearing my conscience. If I couldn't do all the things I had envisioned I'd be doing with my life, if I died and all the things about heaven and hell were true, then I needed to at least relieve my conscience.

Confess.

Acknowledge my mistakes to find absolution.

Well, you get the point.

"You think I'm interesting?" I asked, not waiting for his answer. "Okay, I'll tell you something about me. I have five secrets. Five secrets I don't want to carry with me to the grave. Probably the only five things that don't render me a complete bore."

"You're being melodramatic. It's just a technical glitch. People are—"

"Coming to rescue us. Yeah, got it." I rolled my eyes because I didn't believe a word he said. "Except that it sure felt like an earthquake, and everyone's probably gone."

"Earthquakes happen all the time. And people return for those left behind. So, what are your secrets?"

The air was getting all hot and stuffy because the air conditioning was no longer working. Already my lungs were burning, and my head was dizzy. It was only a matter of time until we ran out of oxygen, and he knew it.

"You want to hear them? Well, I'm scared of dark places. Any dark place," I said. "Always have been, and this is my worst nightmare."

"You don't need to be scared. I'm here. Being stuck in an elevator is not a big deal. And a lot of people are scared of the dark, but once you know it's just in your mind, your imagination, your fear talking, you'll get over it."

I smiled bitterly. "You're great at this. You really are. And if I had to go through this all over again and I could choose one person to be stuck in an elevator with, it'd probably be you. But that doesn't change anything. I'm still scared out of my mind. It's—"

"Nyctophobia."

"Yeah, that."

In the darkness, I could feel the smile on his lips, and for a moment I took the time to imagine him. But all that came out was a fuzzy picture of blue eyes and a soft, sexy smile.

Maybe lopsided.

Or dimples, because I was a sucker for those.

"What's number two?" His voice was hoarse now. Definitely trouble breathing.

"I'm buried in student and credit card loans. It's so bad, it's unreal. Last week I said to my best friend Jude that if I didn't get this interview, I'd fake my resume just to get a job. Any job. She laughed about it, but I meant it. I'm really that desperate."

"The depravity of it," Sexy Voice said. Was he mocking me? I had just opened my mouth to speak with a comeback burning on the tip of my tongue when he cut me off. "I think, given the circumstances, it's understandable. It doesn't make you a bad person...unless you pretend to be a dentist. My point is, there's far worse out there."

"Probably." I sucked in a deep breath and regretted it instantly. My head felt so dizzy, I feared I might just pass out. I had to hurry up if I wanted to get to the highlight of my little confession.

"I guess we all revert to lying and cheating if we want to achieve something, because there's no other way to get there. What about the next one?" Sexy Voice said, as though reading my mind.

"You're not bored yet?"

"Not yet. It's definitely getting interesting." His fingers brushed my wrist, and in spite of the macabre of the situation, I found myself relishing his touch, maybe enjoying it a bit more than was proper.

The next point on my little list was a little tricky. "I'm twenty-two, and yet I'm a virgin," I said before I could stop myself.

"Maybe you never found find the right person, or the right situation," he whispered after a slight pause.

I laughed, fighting the need to elaborate. "You have an excuse for everything, don't you?"

"I'm just a realist."

"Or an optimist." With a sexy voice, and a sexy body, and a face I couldn't remember. Too bad we were about to suffocate, or else I might have found myself just a little bit drawn to this one.

The darkness before my eyes began to spin. If it weren't for his strong arms around me, I would have dropped to the floor, too weak to sit up straight. "I might need to cut to the last point on my list," I said. "And it's a big one. I have carried it all my life."

"Hold on to me," he whispered.

I was. More than he'd ever know.

"Someone died because of me." My voice came so low and faint, I wasn't sure he could hear me. "I'll never be able to live with myself."

Silence. For a second, I wondered if he had even heard me.

"I'm sure it wasn't like that. It was an accident," he said at last.

No hesitation.

No blame.

No mistrust.

Either he was a good person and believed in the good in people, or he was trying to keep the conversation light because of our situation, and then sprint for the nearest exit—if we ever made it out alive.

I shook my head. "You don't know me. You know nothing about me."

Another pause. A few seconds passed, during which I could hear his breathing, slow and steady, but slightly labored.

"Lay down," he whispered. "The air's cooler on the floor."

Didn't he hear what I'd just told him? He tugged at my hand, and I did as instructed.

His arms wrapped around me and he drew me to his chest. I nestled in his arms.

The minutes passed, and the alarm continued to blare. With every second, breathing became harder. If out of a lack of oxygen or something else, I couldn't tell.

"No one's coming for us, are they?" I whispered inaudibly, my face buried against his strong chest. He smelled so good it was impossible to resist his scent.

"We should do something to take our mind off it," he whispered. His voice had become quiet, shaky, heavy, and—was that fear?

"What?"

"I could kiss you," he whispered.

His hands cupped my face. I looked up, my gaze searching him in the darkness, when I realized that this might just be our last moment.

I might die with a stranger.

"Laurie?" he asked, his voice drawing me to reality.

"I don't even know your name," I whispered.

He chuckled. "It doesn't matter now, does it?"

No, not really. "I want to kiss you, too."

In a bold moment, I raised my mouth to meet his. He ran a thumb across my lips before our mouths connected, warm and tender. For a second, I could sense his hesitation, and then his lips opened to claim my mouth with a hunger that took my breath away.

The sound of an alarm continued to carry over, but I didn't care. All I wanted were this stranger's lips on mine and the hot waves of want he sent through me, helping me to forget, keeping me alive—on the brink of sanity—with nothing but a kiss. I had never felt this way before. I had never been in such a state of fear and gratitude that I wasn't alone. Then again, I had never been so close to dying.

My fingers tangled in his hair, pulling him closer, our mouths meeting once more, when something hard crashed against the walls, resulting in a loud thud. I turned my head toward the door.

A shrill noise, like metal scratching against metal, echoed, followed by the sound of a different alarm, the noise increasing in volume. I pressed my palms against my ears, and watched how something pried the door open.

"They're here for us," I said, relief streaming through me. He didn't say anything.

"Did you hear what I just said?" I asked again, touching him. "You were right. They came back for us."

Suddenly, a bright light blinded me. I raised my hand to shield my eyes from the blinding brightness.

Arms wrapped around me and pulled me to my feet, and something cold was pressed against my face. I inhaled automatically, then with more fervor as I realized someone was holding an oxygen mask against my mouth and nose.

"I've got her," a male voice yelled in my ear, the sound almost as loud as the blaring in the background. "We're coming out now."

My head snapped back toward the elevator, in the stranger's direction, and I opened my mouth to speak. To my dismay, I realized he wasn't behind me, or maybe I couldn't see him through the thick curtain of charcoal smoke that had filled the hall.

"No. Please help him," I croaked, planting my feet firmly on the ground, but the arms around me were stronger. My voice could barely reach my ears, let alone penetrate the shrill sound of the alarm.

Struggling against the iron grip, I was carried away before I could turn to get a glimpse of the stranger in the elevator. "No," I pleaded. "Please. You've got to help him. Please."

But my voice was too weak to get anyone's attention.

As I was carried down flights and flights of stairs, I glimpsed more people being helped out—their faces reflecting their shock and disbelief. Figuring someone might need it more than I did, I tried to remove the oxygen mask, but my rescuer pressed it against my mouth, his gesture urging me forcefully to keep it on. Eventually we burst through the reception area and onto the street outside, where hundreds of evacuated office workers and onlookers had gathered, some filming the event on their cell phones, others commenting loudly.

"I'm fine," I said to a concerned woman and scanned the faces around me, even though I knew better than to expect a miracle.

My heart was slamming so hard against my chest, I was sure it would break. If the stranger had been rescued, he couldn't possibly find me in the crowd, not least because we hadn't exchanged names. We didn't even know what the other person looked like. As I was guided to the waiting medical assistance, a crashing sound rang behind me so loud that the rumble rocked my body and the ground beneath my feet vibrated. A cloud of dust billowed into the sky.

My heart stopped.

"The library," a woman in the crowd shouted. "It's the library. It's gone."

"The whole floor's collapsed."

"People are still trapped inside," a fireman shouted into what looked like a radio, and began to gesticulate. "Send another unit. I repeat, send another unit. We need as many people as possible."

Oh, my god.

I stared at the building, my fingers clasped over my mouth in shock as the disaster unfolded. I didn't know if he had survived, but I hoped he was safe. That he had made it out in time. Chances were slim. I realized if he didn't survive, he'd be my sixth secret—the man with the sexy voice whose name I didn't know.

End of sample

To those, who want to learn more about Brooke's past
and the story behind the Lucazzone estate, I welcome
you to read the prequel trilogy to No Exceptions:

SURRENDER
YOUR LOVE
J.C.REED

A THANK YOU LETTER

This story couldn't have been done without the many amazing people in my life.

A huge thank-you to my readers and Facebook for supporting me through trying times.

Thank you for being the best fans any author could want.

Thank you all for giving the Surrender Your Love trilogy and the No Exceptions series a chance. This book wouldn't exist without you.

J.C. Reed

Connect with me online:

My website: http://www.jcreedauthor.blogspot.com

Facebook: http://www.facebook.com/pages/AuthorJCReed

Twitter: http://www.twitter.com/jcreedauthor

THE LOVER'S SURRENDER

Made in the USA
San Bernardino, CA
29 April 2016